About the Author

Rebecka Andersson is a Swede who writes books in English (don't ask why). It's really a hobby of hers (her day job includes writing as well, but that's a different matter) and this book is a result of that hobby. It's also her second published work overall.

It's a Challenging Thing

Rebecka Andersson

It's a Challenging Thing

Vanguard Press

VANGUARD PAPERBACK

© Copyright 2024
Rebecka Andersson

ISBN 978 1 80016 973 9

Vanguard Press is an imprint of
Pegasus Elliot Mackenzie Publishers Ltd.
www.pegasuspublishers.com

First Published in 2024

Vanguard Press
Sheraton House Castle Park
Cambridge England

Printed & Bound in Great Britain

A big thank you to everyone who has helped getting this
book published.

Whoops!

The lunch had been scrumptious, and the evening meal promised to be more so, including a delightful pudding. But before that happened....

"Right, come on then, lessons await!"

She groaned internally at those words but obediently followed to the room that served as a classroom.

Her mentor, Tanya, took up her place by the blackboard as she herself sat down at the desk, opening her notebook.

Problem was that the subject didn't hold her interest for long and soon enough she was doodling in the notebook rather than listening. A loud sigh slipped out as she felt more and more bored by the minute.

Her mentor glared at her and gestured meaningfully at the blackboard with a raised eyebrow. In response she groaned and put her head down at the desk.

There was a chuckle above her, and her hair was ruffled. Her head shot up, startled.

"How did you get there so fast?"

"Magic. You know, the thing you're supposed to be learning," her mentor said emphatically, a small smirk playing on her face.

"I know. But we've been doing theory forever. It's dull! When can we do real stuff?" She whinged, giving her mentor a pout.

"Theory is important. How can you make something if you don't understand it?"

She pouted harder and her mentor rolled her eyes, giving up.

"Fine. Learning by observing then. Let's go to the lab."

She cheered and followed her mentor eagerly. The lab was one of the most interesting rooms in the house. She had only been there a few, short times and loved it down there.

She helped to put the cauldron in place and watched admiringly as her mentor easily lit a fire under it with a wave of her hand. Then the potion-making started.

It was a pretty simple potion and she helped with the steps, even noting them down. Tanya seemed very pleased by that.

The lab served as a lab as well as a storage space. A large bookshelf by the wall happened to contain several magical items that she was itching to explore, something her mentor rarely allowed. But today she got her chance as her mentor needed to go to the bathroom and the potion was to simmer for ten minutes. And as her mentor disappeared up the stairs she shot to the bookshelf. It had all sorts of knick-knacks and interesting stuff on it, and she proceeded to take in everything, fingers itching to pick up something and look at it closer.

A glimmer caught her eye and she curiously picked up a chain with a locket on it. It seemed to shimmer in the light from the fire. As she pondered what could be so magical about what looked like an ordinary necklace there was a swooping sensation in her belly.

"Whoops!" she squeaked as she was whisked away.

Swept away

It felt as if she was spinning. Very quickly, quicker than she'd ever spun before. And as she landed, right on her backside, she promptly threw up.

It took her a while to recover. And as she shakily stood up, she carefully looked around. There were people everywhere and some were staring at her openly. Others seemed to be in too much of a hurry to take notice of anything around them. She didn't like the staring people, and when a few of them started to approach her, she bolted.

They didn't seem to be following her, so she slowed down after a bit. Subtly taking in her surroundings as she walked, she quickly concluded that she had no idea where she was. That thought scared her and she stumbled. As she did so the locket fell out of her hand. She watched it come to a stop and saw a hand pick it up. The owner of the hand examined it before he looked at her, a glint in his eye that made her very uncomfortable.

"Magic, hm?" he said.

"Give it back!" she demanded, her voice shaking slightly.

"I could, if you tell me what you need it for." He walked closer to her as he talked.

"It's mine!" was the only response she could come up with.

"Finders keepers," he mocked.

"You can't have found it if I didn't lose it, I just dropped it," she growled, frustrated and feeling very nervous.

"Fair enough." He held out the locket as if to give it to her, but as she reached for it, he pulled back. "Tell me where you found it first."

"I don't owe you any explanations," she snarled.

"Guess I'll just keep it then," and made as if to walk away.

She rushed at him, snatching the locket out of his hand before he had time to react. Then she ran, hoping to lose him in the crowd. He was quick though and followed her. She sped away, rounding a corner and came to a stop by a tall wall. It was a dead end. As he approached her with a smug smile on his face she screamed.

"Leave me alone!"

A bolt of energy shot out of her, then the swooping sensation came again and whisked her off.

*

She was prepared as she landed this time and didn't fall. Her feet hurt badly though as they slammed into the ground.

She looked around, there was a house nearby and two faces staring out the window at her. There was no one else around, and they looked close to her age, so she hoped she could handle it if they tried to attack.

The faces disappeared from the window and two seconds later the front door flew open, and they rushed towards her. She backed away a few steps and took up a protective stance. They took the hint and didn't try to come closer.

"Hi," the girl said excitedly.

"Hello," she said cautiously.

"That was really cool. How did you just appear like that?" the girl asked, staring intensely at her.

"Obviously she has magic," the boy said arrogantly giving the girl a look as if it should have been obvious.

"So, what if I do?" she asked defensively, giving the boy a distrustful look.

The boy caught the look and started to stutter. The girl snorted slightly and shook her head:

"Ignore my brother, he's just a know-it-all who likes to lecture people."

The boy gave his sister a sour look, and suddenly the girl had grasped her arm and started to drag her to the house.

"Come on, tell me all about yourself."

She was practically shoved onto a sofa and the girl sat next to her as the brother sat gently, carefully on the other side of her.

"What's your name?" the girl asked.

Names were power, and even though these kids didn't seem to have any magical powers she was reluctant to give it to them.

"Tell me yours first," she challenged.

"Right, sorry. I'm Chloe, and this is Leo, my brother," Chloe said, gesturing at her brother.

"I'm… Sarah," she lied, not exactly her name, but close enough.

"Nice to meet you," Chloe grinned, shaking her hand enthusiastically as Leo mumbled the same words.

Sarah gave a small, insecure smile, feeling very out of her depth and part of her wanted to excuse herself.

"How old are you?" Chloe asked.

"Twelve. And you?" she returned the question out of politeness.

"Eleven," Chloe answered, looking very proud.

Leo cleared his throat pointedly and Chloe blushed, glaring at her brother:

"Fine, I'm ten. I'll be eleven in a few days. Leo has another two months to go." Her tone sounded slightly mocking, but it didn't seem sincere.

Leo rolled his eyes.

"I'll fetch something to drink. Do you like raspberry soda?" he asked.

"Sure," she responded.

She had never actually tried it before, but she liked the taste of raspberries and thought it would be interesting to try soda.

*

The sugar and the bubbles made Sarah giggly, and she felt more relaxed after a few sips, answering questions more easily.

"Do you live alone?" she asked, having been taken on a tour around the house and seeing no adults around.

"No, mum and dad are at work," Chloe answered.

"Shouldn't you be in school? It's the middle of the day, and autumn," she said.

"The teachers had a meeting, so we got a day off." Chloe sounded very happy about that.

"I see," as she took another sip of the soda.

There was silence for a while, until Leo spoke up:

"What about your parents? Will they show up out of the blue, too?"

"Oh, no, I live with Tanya. She's my mentor," Sarah explained.

Then she proceeded to tell them how she had ended up where she was now. They listened interestedly and as she finished Chloe asked.

"Have you tried wishing, really hard?"

Sarah just stared at her quizzically, having no idea what she was talking about.

"We... uh... we had an interesting experience with a wishing rock a few months ago," Leo explained, tugging slightly at his earlobe and looking awkward.

"Ah," Sarah said, understanding completely, having read about the subject a while back. "But this isn't a rock though, I don't think it'll work," she said apologetically.

"Does it hurt to try?" Chloe asked.

Grumbling and feeling rather ridiculous, Sarah took the locket out of her pocket and held it with both hands, then she closed her eyes and made a wish. As she suspected, nothing happened, and a wave of disappointment swept over her. Chloe made a disappointed noise and Leo sighed.

"Well, it was worth a try. How about you stay here, our parents might be able to help you get home."

"Yes, please," Sarah said feelingly, knowing it was her best option and hoping intensely that Leo was right about their parents being able to help.

After just sitting in silence for ten minutes Sarah became restless and got off the sofa. As she passed the window, she noticed someone walking towards the house.

"There is someone coming this way."

"Probably Tommy, our neighbour. Since our adventure with the wishing stone our parents don't like to leave us alone and has Tommy checking up on us during the day when they're at work," Leo said.

Chloe got up from the couch and walked to Sarah:

"Hey, maybe Tommy can help you?" Chloe said excitedly.

Sarah's eyes widened as she realised what the man was holding, and a wave of terror swept over her as his eyes met hers

"I have to go," she murmured, backing away from the window.

"Why?" Leo asked.

At the same time Chloe said with a frown. "Oh, it's not Tommy. It's Reginald."

"He's a magic hunter," Sarah explained, looking around for a possible exit.

Leo swore, and Chloe started to lead her towards the kitchen door as the front door slammed open. Sarah made a gagging noise as the necklace she always wore was grabbed and she was pulled backwards. She could hear Chloe and Leo shouting, and she jerked to the side in an attempt to get free. As she did so the chain on her necklace snapped, and she wasted no time in fleeing to the kitchen and out the door. She ran as fast as she could into the nearby woods. The swooping sensation came again, and this time she felt grateful as she was whisked away.

Getting more lost

As she landed, she sank immediately to the ground and the feeling of gratitude gave way to nausea and a sense of despair. The nausea grew, and she had to throw up for the second time that day. As she finished, she buried her face in her hands and started to cry.

She felt so stupid. If she had thought of it, she could have used her necklace to communicate with Tanya; there was a charm on it that allowed communication. And now it was too late, her necklace was probably lost forever. And so were her chances of getting home.

As her tears subsided, she looked up and was shocked to discover that it was dark. She couldn't see a thing.

When her eyes adjusted, she realised she was in a cellar. That scared her because it was quite clear that someone lived there. She also felt a slight sense of shame as she remembered being sick.

A sharp voice interrupted her thoughts and startled her:

"Who's there?"

"Someone who came here by accident," she answered shakily.

There was a moment of silence.

"Well, come up here then," the voice said, sounding less sharp.

Carefully and wearily, she walked through the rather messy cellar and up the stairs. There was an older lady standing there, leaning heavily against the wall.

"Hi," Sarah mumbled, glancing up through her fringe at the lady.

"Come with me!" the lady demanded and led the way to the kitchen.

Sarah walked behind her, noticing how almost every step she took was heavy and accompanied by a sharp, but quiet, breath. She wondered if the lady was okay but didn't dare ask.

As they entered the kitchen the first thing she noticed was the sink full of dirty dishes. The lady led her to a big cupboard and opened it. The cupboard was full of cleaning supplies.

The lady gestured to it and said, "You might as well make yourself useful. Start cleaning!"

Frantic search

Tanya urgently needed the bathroom. Leaving her apprentice and the potion in the lab she quickly went up the stairs. She wasn't worried, the potion was of a gentle nature and couldn't blow up unless one did something horribly wrong with it, like throwing in volatile ingredients. And her apprentice had been lectured enough time not to do something like that (unlike Tanya herself, who had been too curious for her own good when she was young).

Her belly was upset, so the bathroom visit took longer than she would have preferred. When she finally was done, she went back to the lab, feeling a sense of relief that everything seemed to be in order except for the fact that her apprentice was missing.

She sighed and rolled her eyes. Her apprentice had a habit of playing hide and seek at times when she was bored. Making sure the potion was still simmering lightly she set out on the hunt, not really minding the game.

Checking all around the lab she frowned.

"Sera!" she called out.

No answer, and she went upstairs to check Sera's regular hiding places. Not finding her there she started looking properly, carefully.

After looking for some time she started to get worried. Returning to the stairs to the lab she called out:

"Seraphina!"

Using a tone of voice her apprentice knew not to ignore, combined with using her apprentice's full name, was usually guaranteed to get an immediate response. She was also using a spell that projected her voice throughout the house.

Nothing happened, and Tanya's heart started to beat quicker. The possibility of Sera lying hurt somewhere, unable to answer crossed her mind and soon she was checking every nook and cranny of the house. She even went outside to check everywhere in the garden.

No results. With a groan she remembered the potion and hurried back to the lab to deal with that before continuing her search.

Luckily, nothing untoward had happened as she was away, and the potion was still just shimmering slightly. Quickly, she dosed the fire underneath the cauldron. Then she scanned the room carefully, hoping to find clues. Her eyes were drawn to the shelf, and to what was missing on it.

"No," she gasped and ran to the shelf to make sure her eyes weren't fooling her.

She groaned as she realised it was true. She started pacing up and down the lab, not sure what to do. Her apprentice could be anywhere, and it was her fault. All because she hadn't got rid of that blasted thing.

That was when she remembered the necklace. The charm on the necklace Sera was wearing was technically half of a charm. Tanya had the other half around her neck, and it was a communication device, but also a location device. It should be able to help her find Sera.

Rushing up the stairs once more she quickly found the book with the location spell. Taking a deep breath, she made sure to focus. Thinking about Sera and feeling the charm in her hand she pronounced the words slowly and clearly. There was a jerking sensation, and she was on her way.

*

She landed inside a house. And there were three people fighting a metre away from her, two children and one adult. She froze all of them with a quick hand gesture. Creating a bit of distance between them, she released them from the spell and fixed them with a glare:

"What are you doing? Where is Sera?" she demanded.

"Magic user!" the adult man cried, pointing at her with a trembling finger. Everything about him screamed magic hunter.

The children exchanged a look and then looked at her:

"Sera? She said her name was Sarah," the girl exclaimed.

Tanya barely paid attention, her eyes locked on the magic hunter, daring him to move. Her eyes went to the broken necklace in his hand and her heart started pounding faster:

"What have you done to her?" she snarled.

Her magic reacted to her anger and everyone's hair suddenly stood up.

"She disappeared, but when I find her, I'll…" Tanya interrupted his speech by binding and gagging him.

"What happened?" she asked the children, grabbing Sera's necklace from the man's hand.

"He tried to grab her, she ran out and we stopped him from getting to her. I didn't see where she went," the girl said apologetically.

"Where are your parents?" Tanya asked next.

"Working," the boy answered.

Tanya nodded slowly, glancing at the magic hunter:

"I suggest you contact them."

*

It took a while to sort everything out. The children's' parents came home almost two hours after being phoned. And the guardians had taken the magic hunter away. Tanya had stiffened as he told the guardians that she was a magic user, but thankfully they had been much more interested in what the children had said about him. That, accompanied by the bruises on their arms and faces, had convinced them of the man's guilt.

Tanya was lost. She didn't know what to do next. The necklace had been the only way to find her apprentice, and now she had nothing to trace Sera with. Magical signatures were hard to trace, especially the signature of someone so young. It was easier to trace someone who had more control of their magic, as the control made the magic more distinct. And tracing magic had never been her strength.

Tanya sighed and stood up, knowing what she had to do.

"Thank you for the tea, Monica, Ben. I'll take my leave now," she said to Chloe and Leo's parents.

"You'll find her, right?" Chloe asked anxiously.

"Yes," Tanya answered, determined, she would not give up until Sera was found, and safe.

"Good, we would love to meet her again," Leo said.

Tanya nodded, patting her pocket with the note containing contact information to the children and their parents.

She gave a bow, gave her goodbyes, and magically transported herself home to grab a few things before going to the one person she hoped could help her.

Helping out

Sarah, which was what she had decided to call herself for now, was confused. The old lady had had her cleaning every room in the small house. She hadn't asked how Sarah had come to be in her house, nor did she seem very worried about it. And Sarah couldn't understand why.

Not that she was going to point it out in case she got thrown out. The thought of being out all alone in an unknown location was too scary to think about.

Her grumbling belly made her realise how late it was. It was well past teatime if the sun was anything to go by. So, she got up from the livingroom floor and went in search of the lady.

The lady was sitting by the small kitchen table, eyes closed, and lips pressed tightly together, her whole body pretty much screaming in pain.

"Should I start tea?" Sarah asked carefully, not wanting to startle the lady.

The lady was startled anyway, though she didn't open her eyes. She made a small gesture with her hand which Sarah took as permission to start cooking.

The cupboards and fridge didn't have all that much, but they weren't bare, and there were plenty of vegetables that Sarah assumed came from the lady's garden. That combined with her limited cooking skills made her decide on a potato and leek soup, which she soon had cooking. She managed to find some bread to go with it.

There was a small pouch in her pocket, a pouch she always carried with her. But even though it looked small on the outside, it was rather big on the inside. It was originally meant for herbs, with different compartments for different herbs. But there was room for more practical things too, like tools and money, a tin bowl and spoon and even sewing supplies.

Right now, Sarah had one herb in mind, one that the pouch had an abundance of. She took it out, crushed the petals and sprinkled it into the bowl meant for the lady.

The two ate in silence, the lady with stiff, slow movements and Sarah practically inhaling her food. As she finished, she looked towards the pot where there was some soup left. Then she looked to the lady. Before she could ask...

"It's yours," the lady said with a dismissive wave, the movement less slow than before.

Sarah got the last of the soup and ate it quickly, finishing the meal with a piece of bread.

The rest of the evening was spent in the living room. The lady was reading and had offered Sarah to choose a book from her bookshelf. Sarah had obligingly picked one out, but she was starting to feel rather anxious and restless and couldn't get into the story.

It was starting to get dark out and she had no idea where she was. All she knew was that this lady seemed to live alone in a forest, judging by the views from the windows and that was not comforting. And she was so tired, the events of the day having caught up with her. If the lady decided to throw her out now, she had no idea what she would do.

She was startled out of her thoughts by the lady:

"What's your name by the way?"

"S…Sarah," she stuttered, not prepared for the question and almost slipped, but managed not to give her real name.

"I'm Ethel. Ethel Thorpe."

"How do you do." Sarah smiled weakly.

"So, it's getting late. I have a spare bedroom you can use. It's not big, and the bed is not in the best shape, but it should do for the night. Then tomorrow we can figure how to get you back to where you belong."

Sarah's heart had started to pound heavily as Ethel had started speaking, but it calmed down as Ethel continued. Now she stared at her, her eyes watering slightly and relief flooding her:

"R…really? You'll help me? Thank you… Thank you so much,"

Ethel pointed out the direction to the bedroom and soon enough Sarah was in a slightly dusty room with an old bed. It creaked as she lay down in it. But she didn't care, her eyes closing almost as soon as her head hit the pillow.

Sarah was up bright and early the next morning, preparing breakfast. She was excited about the possibility of going home. It had been less than a day since she had been swept away from home, but it felt like a week, and she just wanted to go back.

As Ethel came into the kitchen, she looked pleasantly surprised at the made table and freshly brewed tea. Sarah smiled back, a genuine smile, and they sat to eat.

Suddenly the front door was thrown open and Sarah was startled, falling off her chair in surprise. Ethel didn't seem surprised at all, she just gave an annoyed look in the direction of the door and helped Sarah off the floor. Sarah absently noticed that Ethel seemed very agile today and her body didn't seem to pain her anymore.

A young, bespectacled man entered the kitchen. He smiled at Ethel and then looked at Sarah with a raised eyebrow:

"Another lost soul?"

Ethel nodded and gestured at the table:

"Sit!" she commanded.

The man sat down and grabbed a slice of bread. Sarah was confused. She figured he was a regular visitor of Ethel's, but he made it sound as if finding strangers in her house was a regular occurrence.

They ate in silence for a while. Sarah felt very awkward whilst Ethel and the man seemed perfectly content.

"Have you finally seen a doctor about your pain, Auntie?" the man asked Ethel, completely out of the blue Sarah thought.

"No, no. My little guest helped me. A regular little witch, that one," Ethel answered, glancing briefly at Sarah as she spoke.

Sarah's whole body tensed up and she prepared to run. But to her surprise the man turned towards her with a grin, which faded slightly as he saw her fear:

"Whoa! Calm down, kid. I don't care if you're a magic user. You helped my aunt. I'm grateful. Really, thank you."

He sounded sincere, and Sarah felt her body relax slightly.

"What herb did you use anyway?" Ethel asked.

Sarah's face turned towards the lady, the surprise she felt evident on her face. Ethel chuckled.

"Oh honestly, I might be old, but my vision is still good. Do you really think I didn't notice crushed petals in my soup?"

"But… But… why did you eat it?" Sarah gasped; eyes wide at Ethel's lack of preservation skills.

"I am very good at reading people. It's an ability that has served me well when strangers appear in my house. There is nothing about you that makes me suspect you want to hurt me," Ethel answered, her voice kind.

Sarah wasn't entirely sure how to answer that and ended up just staring at Ethel dumbly. Ethel sounded so confident about her people-reading skills, and Sarah had trouble understanding how one could trust a stranger by just looking at them. But before she could ponder the matter further Ethel's nephew spoke up:

"Besides, you're a child, children are automatically granted my aunt's good faith. Now, what herb was it you used?"

He looked very curious. Sarah absently wondered if he was studying medicine or something as she answered:

"Poppies," she muttered.

"Huh, I would have thought belladonna," he said curiously.

Sarah shook her head:

"Poppies are safer."

"Honestly, David, I don't think Sarah wants to answer all your questions. I think she's more interested in going home," Ethel told her nephew reproachfully.

David, which was apparently his name, blushed and nodded. Turning back to Sarah with a more business-like look about him, he asked:

"So, do you know how you came here? Though I think I can guess." The last remark was said with a slight grin.

Sarah answered by taking the locket out of her pocket. David's eyebrows rose.

"Okay, that's not what I expected."

"I don't know what kind of magic this is. It's my mentor's, and when I touched it, it just swept me away,"

Sarah explained, bracing herself in case the locket decided to sweep her off right then and there.

"May I see it?" David asked, reaching towards it.

Sarah wanted to say no, afraid that David would be swept away. But before she could open her mouth, he had already grabbed it. Sarah held her breath, waiting for David to disappear. When a minute had passed with nothing happening, she breathed a sigh of relief.

David was twisting and turning the locket in his hands. He was staring so intently at it his glasses started to slip down his nose. He poked them back in place and huffed in annoyance:

"Well, I have no idea what this is." He said it like he should know it by just looking at it.

"You don't have magic; how could you know it?" Ethel asked drily, her eyes on her knitting needles.

Sarah hadn't noticed when Ethel had taken those out, and it distracted her for a moment. David pouted:

"I thought I could figure it out. I've figured out magical problems before." His tone reminded Sarah of a cranky child.

Ethel got to her feet, shaking her head and looking amused:

"I'll go make some more tea."

"I'll help you," David said, getting to his feet as well.

Ethel rolled her eyes and aunt and nephew started to argue as they turned to the stove. Sarah wasn't sure why they were squabbling, and she felt uncomfortable witnessing it. She rose from the chair, intent on helping to clear the table when Ethel turned to her:

"You can go to the living room; we'll take care of this and be out in a bit."

Sarah nodded in understanding and turned away. She turned back as David said her name:

"Here," he threw the locket at her.

Sarah fumbled a bit but managed to catch it, then she yelped as the swooping sensation made a return and the kitchen faded around her.

Getting help

Tanya was standing outside a familiar house. The sun was beginning to set as it had taken her longer than she'd thought at home. She had also needed to gather some courage before coming. She hadn't been here in years, and despite her gathered courage it took her a while to raise her hand and knock on the door. Finally, the thought of her apprentice scared and alone in a strange place got her hand moving and she rapped on the door. It opened immediately with no one on the other side, and she rolled her eyes at the theatrics.

She knew this house; it had been partly hers once upon a time when she'd lived here with her mother and the house's current resident as well as her aunt and uncle. So, she knew exactly where to look to find him.

As she approached the dining room a voice boomed out:

"Welcome! To a world of wonder. What brings you here, stranger? Do you need a cure for your ailments? Help to find something lost? A spell to protect you from all evils?"

"Oh, cut it out, will you? I need proper help, not cheap tricks and theatrics," she huffed as she entered the living room.

The man stood next to an unnecessarily big cauldron, green smoke welling up from its opening. He was wearing long, blue robes and a matching pointy hat on his head. He was posing regally, but as he met her eyes, he lost his bearings and almost fell over. A look of surprised joy swept over his face, before he schooled it into a more neutral expression:

"Tanya," he said in a mild voice: "What brings you here?" He sounded a bit apprehensive as he asked.

"I… I need your help. I'm sorry to impose on you at this hour, but I really need help," she explained, hating that she sounded so desperate, even though she was.

He immediately looked concerned, approaching her:

"What's wrong, are you hurt? Are you in trouble?"

"No, no, I'm fine. My apprentice though, Seraphina's her name, is missing. And you were always so good at finding people…" she trailed off, biting her lip, looking at him with wide, hopeful eyes.

"Your apprentice?" His eyebrows rose in surprise and there was an amused glint in his eyes.

"Yes," she snapped defensively. "Why is that so funny?"

He shrugged slightly.

"Never thought you were the mentoring type that's all."

Tanya gave him an odd look, not knowing how to respond to that. But then she realised that wasn't important right now:

"Whatever, will you help me find her or not?"

"Yes, yes, of course. Have seat, let's see if we can figure this out."

*

It was difficult. Tanya was frustrated. Since the locket that had swept Sera away was a product of old magic, with a little bit of Tanya's own magic that had been absorbed by it, a search for a magical signature only found Tanya herself. Since Tanya didn't have any objects Sera's magic had created (they had a long way to go in the lessons before Sera could try to create something out of magic) there was no possibility to search for that. And the crystal ball gave no results, not that Tanya had believed it would.

She was so worried, and that in turn made her angry that nothing worked to find Sera. Her anger had already made a few silly hats lying around her blow up.

"Tanya, calm down! Look, it's late, you have used a lot of magic and gone to a lot of places today. You need rest!"

"No, I need to find her!"

"Which will be easier to do after a nap. One hour, okay? Just lie down and shut your eyes for one hour. I will wake you then. And I will continue working until then."

"Luka…"

"Please!" Luka interrupted.

Tanya nodded in defeat. Soon enough she was lying on the soft sofa Luka had in the room. She fell asleep immediately.

*

She woke up to the smell of food, pancakes to be exact. Looking at the clock she shot up, running into the kitchen where Luka was standing by the stove, dressed in regular clothes and making pancakes.

"I've been asleep for five hours!"

"Yes, and don't you feel much better?" Luka sounded more upbeat than he had any right to, Tanya thought.

"You said you'd wake me after one!" she reminded him accusingly.

He glanced at her, looking a bit embarrassed.

"I tried, but you wouldn't wake up. I tried every ten minutes for about an hour, but you just grumbled at me and turned away. Then I… I sat down for a bit in the armchair and managed to fall asleep as well. I'm sorry."

She sighed:

"Suppose I can't blame you for that."

They sat down to eat, both being silent for a while before Luka spoke:

"Does… does Seraphina have ginger hair, hazel eyes and a mark on her hand that looks like a crudely drawn heart?"

Tanya looked at him suspiciously:

37

"Yes," she said slowly, drawing the word out.

He paled and gulped, words coming out of his mouth in a quick pace:

"I think I met her yesterday. She just appeared on the pavement, and I could sense magic. I followed her, and she dropped what looked like a necklace. I picked it up and recognised it immediately. I thought she had stolen it from you. She ran when I started to question her and when I cornered her, she shot nettles at me and disappeared."

Tanya just gaped for moment, taking it all in. Then she shrieked:

"What?!"

"I'm sorry," he squeaked.

Tanya wanted to yell at him, maybe curse him, but that wasn't her main priority at the moment. She took a deep breath:

"Well, you're definitely helping me find her now."

He nodded. They kept eating. After a while Luka spoke again, a bit hesitantly:

"Why did you keep it?"

Tanya winced. Luka had tried to persuade her to get rid of the locket several times as it was unreliable and therefore dangerous. It had been in their family for generations and its initial purpose had been forgotten with time. All their mothers knew about it was that it would randomly transport people to random places. Tanya herself had been transported by it the first time it had been shown to them. Luckily, her aunt Yana, Luka's mother, had been able to quickly retrieve her as she had been very skilled at tracing magical signatures, a skill Luka had inherited.

"I suppose I kept it for sentimental reasons," she mumbled.

That was a decision she was sorely regretting now.

The cousins kept eating in, a rather sombre, silence.

From better to worse

Again, she landed inside a house. This was getting tiresome. She wanted to rave and rant at the unfairness of it all. But a hand on her shoulder made her stiffen in fear.

"Hello, dear, I don't think I've seen you around here before. Have you recently moved to the area?"

The hand on her shoulder belonged to a lady, an old lady, with very kind eyes. Sarah felt herself immediately relax, not feeling threatened at all.

"I am not from here. Honestly, I'm not really sure where I am," she answered.

The lady just smiled at her. Sarah smiled back. Then a man walked into the room. Curiously, Sarah didn't feel threatened by him either, he looked just as kind as the lady did.

"A new neighbour?" he asked.

"No dear, just a temporary visitor," the lady answered.

Before anything else could be said there was a noise from the hallway. Sarah immediately stiffened at the voices:

"I'm telling you, there was a magical burst from here," a creaky voice said.

"Mr and Mrs Jones aren't magical, and I don't think they'll appreciate us just bursting into their house," a frantic voice said in response to the first voice.

A moment later the owners of the voices entered the room. One was a girl who looked to be Sarah's age, and the other was a...

"Hag!" Sarah hissed.

Somehow, she managed to summon the knife from her pouch to her hand. But before she could do anything with it the older man grabbed it from her:

"Now young lady, there will be no fighting in this house, especially involving weapons. Flo is not a threat!"

Sarah lowered her hand, the man's stern tone overpowering her instincts to attack the threat. The girl was staring at her with huge eyes and the hag looked... happy?

"Um..." Sarah started.

"It's an adorable little witch!" The hag exclaimed.

Suddenly the hag had her in a bone-crushing embrace. Sarah floundered, gasping for breath. Just as suddenly the hag let go of her and she almost fell to the floor but managed to find her footing.

*

The man and lady had introduced themselves as Mr and Mrs Jones, the girl's name was Aderyn and she was fourteen years old, and the hag was apparently named Flo. Sarah had apologised for her first reaction towards Flo.

Aderyn had seemed suspicious of Sarah at first but had warmed to her and was now chatting animatedly about her many siblings. Sarah listened attentively, feeling rather awed by how happy Aderyn seemed to be living with so many people. In her own experience living with a lot of people around was tiring and frustrating at the best of times, though she supposed it was different if the people were siblings. Aderyn claimed to enjoy the constant company. She admitted that it was unusual that she managed to spend time alone with Flo and had only managed it today because she had left school early when she felt ill. But she was feeling better now because of Flo. It was apparent after one minute that Flo was a very affectionate being who acted more like an eccentric aunt than a bloodthirsty monster. She apparently lived with Aderyn and her family, in the attic, something that made Sarah gape. But in her advanced age Flo was closer to human than hag and wasn't interested in typical hag activities or had a hag's typical appetite. And Flo seemed to be beloved by everyone who lived in the neighbourhood.

It made Sarah smile. This seemed like a very accepting neighbourhood with a lot of kind people. It was nice to know that there were places like this in the world.

She was so caught up in the story Aderyn was telling about a prank her and some of her siblings had played on the neighbour children that she didn't notice what she was doing with her hands. It wasn't until the now familiar, swooping sensation entered her belly that she realised what she was holding.

*

It was snowing all around her. She put up a hand to protect her eyes from the stingingly cold flakes. Shivering, she tried to look around for anywhere to get some shelter. But the snow fell so thickly it obscured her vision almost completely. So, she stood there frozen, figuratively and kind of literally, for a while with no clue what to do next. Then she looked at the locket that was the cause of all this and growled:

"This is your fault, you stupid thing! Now get me away from this freezing hole!"

The swooping sensation came again.

*

As her feet met solid ground she screamed and threw the locket away from herself. Tears she hadn't been able to shed earlier welled up in her and a strangled sob made it out of her mouth. Frustration was the only feeling in her body.

"Well, well, well, look what we have here," a voice said not far from her.

She became aware of her surroundings then as a dirty shoe stepped on the locket. Distantly, she registered she was in some kind of alley as her eyes travelled upwards from the shoe. The owner of the shoe was a skinny man with a sharp face. It rather reminded her of a rat, beady eyes and all.

"It's a little witch methinks," the rat-man said, apparently the owner of the voice that had spoken before. It was a very unpleasant voice.

"Oh, the boss will be pleased with this one," a gravelly voice said.

She stiffened, that voice had come from behind her. She spun around only to come face to face with a burly man, his face reminding her of a bull's, he even had a nose ring like the bulls in her storybooks.

The bull-man gripped her shoulder tightly, and the rat-man came up behind her and gripped her other shoulder. She swallowed, realising the trouble she was in.

Finding clues

This was incredibly frustrating. Waiting for Luka to get a "feel" for locations of her used magic took a long time and required him to sit completely still with his eyes closed, one hand held out. Meanwhile she had nothing useful to do.

After just sitting and staring at her cousin for a while she decided to look around the house. A wave of nostalgia washed over her as she entered the dining area and got a proper look. Sure, Luka put on his little shows in there, but the walls looked the same; impeccable woodcarvings on the wall which her aunt had kept dust free all the time. Tanya dragged her hand along the patterns, noting a thin layer of dust as she did.

She continued to the office, a room she rarely got to see as a child, and she had been forbidden to enter it after her uncle disappeared. It looked just as she remembered it, nothing had changed since the disappearance. It was completely untouched. Luka clearly didn't use it. There was a layer of dust on every surface. She turned around in the doorway, not wanting to enter it.

She walked up the stairs where the bedrooms were. Her old room looked the same, maybe a bit cleaner than she had left it. Her aunt's bedroom was the same, though dusty. Seeing it made her feel sad and she turned to peer into Luka's room. That one looked different. It was redecorated and looked more like an adult's room than a teenager's, with a soft green colour scheme, a big bed with dark blue sheets, a dark wooden shelf full of books, and a matching wooden desk. Then there was her mother's old room. The bed was the same, and the nightstand. The rest of the room was pretty bare, save for a potted flower on the windowsill. An unexpected lump formed in her throat, and she quickly moved on to the family room, the room she had spent a lot of time in with Luka. The door was stuck, and she had to pull hard on the handle to open it, then she gasped. The room looked like it had been trashed: the shelves were a pile of planks in the corner, the table was standing on three legs, the wallpaper was in pieces. The only thing that was mostly whole in there was the sofa.

"Tanya?" came Luka's voice from downstairs.

She jolted and hurriedly closed the door and went downstairs.

"I've found a trace," Luka said with a slight smile.

Tanya gave one back:

"Then let's go!"

Luka grabbed her hand and off they went.

*

They landed inside a house, a fact that made Tanya very nervous as it felt like they were breaking in. But before she could do anything a young man entered the room.

"Oh, hello," he said, not seeming bothered at all that two strangers were standing in his kitchen.

"Hi," Tanya said slowly, "sorry to just appear like this. It's a long story… You wouldn't have seen a young girl around, would you?"

"You mean Sarah?"

"Yes! Is she here?" Tanya asked, anxiously.

"No, I'm sorry. She was here a few hours ago and then she just vanished into thin air.

The hope that had bloomed in Tanya was washed over by a wave of disappointment. Before she could tell Luka to continue searching another voice spoke up:

"Well, who's this then?"

"I don't know auntie, they haven't introduced themselves yet, but they're looking for Sarah," the young man answered the older woman who was standing in the doorway.

Tanya felt herself blushing slightly at her lack of manners. But any answer she was about to give was thrown off at the woman's suspicious look:

"And why are you looking for Sarah?"

The young man was now looking at her suspiciously as well and looked her over as if he was looking for something. Then he did the same to Luka. Tanya met the woman's gaze, befuddled.

What are they suspicious about? she thought.

Suddenly a vase on the windowsill blew up and everyone looked at Luka who looked rather embarrassed. Tanya acted on instinct and fixed the vase quickly.

"You're magic," the young man exclaimed.

Tanya tensed, ready to run, and saw out of the corner of her eye her cousin assuming a fighting stance.

The woman didn't look suspicious anymore and gave them a friendly smile:

"Well, you're definitely not magic hunters."

Tanya was immediately offended.

"Of course not!"

"Good, that's good. Would you like some tea? I've just brewed some."

Tanya and Luka looked at each other, neither feeling keen on it, but it seemed like a good idea to get some information out of these two.

*

"Your little girl was extremely helpful. Even though I practically ordered her to clean in here she didn't protest or grumble. And as you can see, it's spotless," Ethel gushed.

Tanya smiled and took another sip of tea, thinking about Sera's room at home which she only cleaned after a lot of nagging. And Ethel was right, the house did seem quite clean.

"And not only that, but she also helped with auntie's pains. I'm extremely glad and grateful that she did, as auntie hates doctors," David continued.

It was obvious that her apprentice had made a good impression on them, and they seemed distraught that she had vanished as she had.

"Speaking of whom, we should continue looking," Tanya said, standing up from the sofa.

Luka nodded and stood up stiffly:

"Quite, I have found another trace. Thank you for the tea." He bowed and avoided eye contact as he spoke.

He grabbed Tanya's shoulder, and just before they disappeared Ethel called out:

"Please come back when you find her, I'll just worry otherwise."

Tanya didn't have time to respond.

Into, and out of, the cage

Sarah was honestly terrified but tried not to show it. The men who had captured her had tied up her hands and were currently dragging her by the end of the rope she was tied up with. They were walking in front of her, chatting easily and behaving like dragging someone through the desert was something they did every day.

After they had caught her in the alley, they had tied her up and thrown her into a vehicle. She had tried to use her magic, but it had been no use and one of them had condescendingly informed her that the vehicle was protected against magic. After riding for a short while they had stopped, and she had been untied enough so she'd be able to walk. Which led to where they were now in the desert. They had been walking for at least two hours, though she found it hard to keep track of time in her current situation. And she was parched. Part of her wanted to fall to the ground, both from the thirst and because her body felt very achy. But she forced herself to move her feet, not wanting to find out what these men would do if she stopped moving.

Eventually they came to the top of a small, sandy hill and Sarah gaped at the terrifying view before her. Before she could react, there was a sharp tug at the rope around her hands and she stumbled. Fortunately, she managed to find her balance and followed them down.

As they approached what she had seen from the hilltop the fear grew even more inside her. There were cages, rather large ones, with people in them. A few metres away there was a small platform, obviously assembled in a rush and not looking very structurally sound. With a sinking heart Sarah realised what the plans for her were and just what was happening in this place.

By the witches and wizards of old, I'm being sold! she thought, terror gripping her.

As she was shoved into a cage she quickly moved away from the door and the bars of the cage. Then she moved to a small, unoccupied space and sat down, making sure no one could reach her from the outside, and tried to calm down by studying the people around her.

Everyone in the cage seemed to be older than her, and she realised they were all female. A few of them were huddled in little groups whilst others hung around by themselves. There was no eye contact between anyone other than the ones in groups and the atmosphere was, understandably, tense.

After observing everyone for a while she noticed the small figure of a girl in a corner, who looked so lonely, sitting huddled and trembling slightly. Sarah couldn't help but scoot over. Sitting down a little bit away from her, she said a quiet hello.

The startled girl glanced up at her through a short, messy fringe:

"Hi," she answered so quietly Sarah barely heard her.

She's just a kid, Sarah thought, horrified.

"What's your name?" she asked kindly.

"Lou," the girl answered in a whisper.

"I'm Sarah," she whispered back, not wanting anyone else to hear it.

Now that she got a good look, she realised that Lou looked very unkempt, with tattered clothes, face partly covered in filth and small scars and bruises all over.

She can't be older than seven, she thought, feeling more horrified by the second.

Before she could ask Lou anything else an arm appeared from between the cage's bars and grabbed the little girl by the shoulder. The arm belonged to a big man who had an unsettling grin on his face and an evil look in his eyes as he looked at Lou. Lou squeaked, and Sarah growled, throwing herself towards the arm and scratching it viciously, making the man retract it. Then she got herself and Lou away from the man's reach and further away from the bars of the cage, glaring at the man who glared straight back. She tried to will her magic to work, wanting desperately to put a curse on that man and everyone outside the cages. She wanted the cages to disappear and for everybody in them to be safe. But of course, her magic didn't listen.

Suddenly there was a commotion by the cage's opening. One of the men had opened it and a group of women had rushed at him, knocking him out, then they grabbed his knives and guns and ran out of the cage. The other women followed and then everything was chaos. Sarah took advantage of it, grabbed Lou and just ran for it.

*

Running in sand was hard and she absently wondered if it would have been easier with shoes. Lou was huffing and puffing, having trouble keeping up but making a valiant effort. Sarah slowed down eventually as no one seemed to be following them and the site of their capture was a fair distance behind them.

The desert looked to be endless, no shade or water in sight, and Sarah knew they couldn't go on forever like this. She was already feeling a bit faint, the adrenaline that had given her enough energy to escape earlier was starting to fade. She noticed that Lou looked exhausted. Sarah wondered how long Lou had been in that cage, and if they had received food or water in there.

That was when she remembered the oranges. They were in her pouch, put there by her mentor four days ago when Sarah went for her daily walk and Tanya had reminded her that she needed to eat more fruit.

Though she didn't normally care for oranges it really was a sight for sore eyes now. She frowned slightly upon noticing the absence of her knife, but rather than dwelling on that she grabbed her multitool and took out the screwdriver. With a sharp jab the orange soon had a decent hole in it. Holding the orange above her face she squeezed some juice into her mouth. Then she coaxed Lou to do the same and she grimaced at the slightly sour taste of the fruit juice.

Feeling slightly better, the girls continued walking.

The search continues

They landed outside a house. Luka stared at it as if it had offended him:

"The trace comes from inside the house," he muttered.

Tanya knocked at the door and heard footsteps approaching.

"I'll stay out here," Luka mumbled, staring at the ground, hands in his pockets.

The door opened and Tanya froze. The hag who was standing there looked at her curiously. Luka hissed at the sight. But before either of them could do anything the hag exclaimed:

"More witches? Has this house become a beacon? I need to look into that." With that she stepped out and turned to look at the house intently.

"Uh," Tanya and Luka looked at each other, confused.

"Flo? Oh, there you are. Who are you?" A teenage girl came out of the house, looking curiously at the two of them.

"I'm Tanya, and this is Luka. We're looking for my apprentice," Tanya explained.

Luka was wearily staring at the hag, who was apparently named Flo.

"You mean Sarah?" the girl asked.

"Yes."

"Oh, that adorable little girl was here. Appeared out of nowhere and then vanished into thin air," Flo said a tad mournfully.

"Oh," Tanya mumbled, drooping slightly in defeat: "Well, then we should continue looking…"

"Wait!" the girl exclaimed and rushed back into the house.

A moment later she was back, followed by two older people, a man and a woman. The man was holding a knife. Tanya stiffened, prepared to throw up a shield if need be, and then cocked her head slightly. There was something familiar about that knife.

"I believe this belongs to your apprentice," said the man offering her the knife, handle first.

"Thank you." She took it, and then stood there, unsure of how to proceed.

"Would you like to come in for some tea?" the woman asked.

What is it about people's need to offer others tea? Tanya thought to herself, amused despite everything.

"No!" Luka burst out. "I… I mean."

"That is very kind of you, but we must continue our search for Sarah. Thank you for looking after her when she was here," Tanya intervened, giving her cousin a dirty look.

"Please come by when you find her," Flo said, the girl nodding in agreement.

"Of course," Tanya was quick to agree.

Then Luka grabbed her shoulder, and they were off.

*

Snow! There was snow everywhere, from what little she could see. Hastily, she threw up a shield that protected them from the many flakes that were raging around. Squinting, she tried to make out if she could see anything. And she prayed she wouldn't find Sera lying on the cold ground.

As the wind was loud in her ears, she didn't hear Luka as he tried to speak to her. Then she felt his hand on her shoulder, which made her realise how cold it was. They hadn't even been here for five minutes. This made her even more worried about Sera. But before she could panic, she was swept away.

Into the forest

(Day 2-3)

Sarah stared befuddled at the trees in front of her. She couldn't figure it out. It just didn't make sense.

They had been walking in the hot desert for hours, rationing one of the oranges as best they could so they could save the other one for later. Then the sun had started to set and the sand beneath their feet had slowly changed to dirt. In the gloom she had thought she was seeing things, because it seemed so unlikely that a forest would exist so close to a desert. But as they had come closer, she realised her eyes hadn't deceived her. And now they were right in front of the forest.

Lou was grabbing her arm tightly, looking fearfully at the trees. Sarah was indecisive, because on the one hand, the forests of the world were usually dangerous one way or another. On the other hand, there would be a better chance for them to find food and water in a forest than in a desert. And the soft, slightly damp earth felt wonderful on her bare feet, definitely better than scorching sand. And that was what made her decision for her.

Explaining her reasoning to Lou the girl nodded apprehensively. She hadn't spoken at all during the day, other than telling Sarah her name. But then, Sarah hadn't spoken much either, the dryness of her mouth making it incredibly hard to speak.

They entered the forest.

*

It had been good decision. After a little bit of walking, they had come across bushes practically overflowing with berries. They had managed to eat until they were both full, with plenty of berries to spare. Then, as it was getting darker and darker every minute, they agreed to settle for the night.

Lou was out like a light as soon as she laid her head down. Sarah was staring up towards the sky which was visible through the treetops, the stars and moon giving a little bit of light. The silence of the forest unnerved her, and she wished she had a torch. It occurred to her to try to make a fire but seeing as she had no matches she quickly gave up on that idea. She sighed and tried to get comfortable. It was to the memory of her mentor singing while she cooked the other day that she drifted off.

Now what?

"Why did you do that?" Tanya demanded, glaring: "I didn't even have time to see if she was there!"

"I assure you she wasn't," Luka said calmly.

His calm only made her more upset:

"And how would you know? Do you have magic vision that can see everything around you at once?" A small part of her knew she was being ridiculous, but she was too frustrated to care.

"I picked up another trace, which is why we are here," he gestured around them.

It was dark around them; it was probably late at night. And wherever they were didn't smell good.

It appeared to be some kind of alley. Tanya shivered, feeling trapped.

"Have you found another trace?" she asked Luka.

"No. It appears the trail ends here," Luka mumbled.

"How can it? She's not here," Tanya snapped, now extremely worried.

A sudden light made her flinch. But it was only Luka, who had turned on a small torch. She had no idea where he had got it from but was grateful he had had the foresight to bring it as conjuring magic light would have drawn too much attention. He shone the light around the alley and they both looked for clues. Tanya spotted something.

Walking over to a few dustbins she picked it up and her heart dropped at the sight. It was the locket that had taken Sera away in the first place. She showed it to Luka.

"Now what?" she asked.

Unexpected company

(Day 3)

Lou was a very silent girl, it almost seemed as if she was afraid of speaking. She stuck close to Sarah and flinched every time anything around them made a noise.

The place they had settled for the night had become overrun by aggressive squirrels early that morning. Luckily, they had managed to pick plenty of berries to store in Sarah's pouch before the squirrels had started on the berries themselves.

So now they were walking. The forest seemed vast to them. There had been no reason to pick a particular direction since they had no idea where anything was. At least Sarah didn't. If Lou had any clues of their whereabouts she didn't say.

Eventually Sarah grew tired of the silence, and as they sat down to rest and eat a little, she started talking:

"So… Looks like we'll be eating berries for a while. Sorry about that," she cringed at how lame it all sounded.

Lou shrugged:

"I don't mind," she mumbled.

Sarah nodded slowly, not really knowing what to say next. What did kids usually talk about anyway? When she'd been at the sanctuary she hadn't really talked to the other children as she'd preferred her own company to her noisy peers. And ever since she had come into Tanya's care she hadn't really spoken to other children, or other people than Tanya really. The children in the village she'd overheard only seemed to discuss shows they'd seen on the telly or some new gadget they had or wanted. Neither of which she had any experience with, and she doubted Lou had any either.

"What… is your favourite food?" she asked. It was the first question that came to her, hoping to get a conversation going.

Lou glanced at her through her fringe and shrugged. Sarah sighed in defeat and lay down on the ground.

"Let's rest a bit before we continue," she said, closing her eyes.

She heard Lou lying down beside her.

*

She woke suddenly by Lou shaking her and she sat up, confused. Lou pointed to some bushes which were rustling much more than the other bushes around. Sarah got to her feet, getting the multitool out of her pocket and squinting at the bushes. She squared her shoulders, readying herself for a fight. Not that she could do much if there was a ferocious beast in there, but maybe she could scare it away.

The bushes were smaller than her, which meant that hopefully the beast wouldn't be too large in size.

Suddenly something jumped out of the bushes and Sarah blinked. Then she crouched down:

"Hello there, kitty," she smiled, relieved and enchanted by the cute animal. The cat hissed at her, but then it stood up straight and stared intently at her. Sarah stared back as the realisation came to her:

"A familiar."

The cat nodded and almost looked as if it was smiling.

"Do you know how to get to civilisation?"

The cat nodded again and started walking. Smiling, Sarah grabbed Lou's hand and followed it.

*

Apparently, it was a long road to civilisation, and as they stopped for the night the cat suddenly ran off. The girls watched it leave, disappointed. They had grown fond of it quickly. They sat down on the ground and ate a few more berries and a few common chickweeds they had found during the walk. The cat had fed itself, catching a few small rodents during the walk. The girls had turned away as it ate.

Suddenly there was a rustling sound, and the cat was back, holding a few thick twigs in its mouth and looking at Sarah intently. It took her a few seconds to understand what it wanted:

"I… don't know how to make a fire. No matches."

The cat gave her a very judgmental look and she turned away, avoiding its gaze.

"I do," a quiet voice said.

Sarah turned to Lou, wide-eyed. Those were the first words she had spoken that day without prompting. The cat looked pleased and made a gesture with its head towards the twigs. Sarah watched as Lou quickly prepared an area for a fire and then managed to actually light a fire. The three of them settled down around the fire with the cat settling into Lou's lap, much to the girl's delight. Sarah was both impressed by Lou's skills, and a little jealous that the cat chose to cuddle with her.

*

Sarah had trouble sleeping, so she sat up and stared at the fire. She had tried a few easy spells, but her magic didn't seem to work, and it worried her. Lou was lying on the ground with the cat next to her, an arm around the cat.

She was startled out of some deep thoughts as Lou unexpectedly sat up.

"Can't sleep?" she asked.

Lou shook her head in response.

"Me neither," Sarah sighed.

Lou moved to sit next to her, the cat following as if in a sleepwalking state and it immediately lay down in Lou's lap and started purring up a storm. Sarah smiled at the sight. Just as her eyelids started drooping Lou spoke up.

"I don't really have a favourite food. The ship I used to work on… well there wasn't much food to choose from." She was looking at the cat as she spoke, her voice slightly hoarse as she spoke slowly, unsurely.

Sarah put a hand on her shoulder, trying to be comforting. The fact that Lou had been working on a ship was worrying and didn't paint a good picture of what Lou's life had been like so far, especially considering where she had ended up.

The purring of the cat was the only noise for a while until Sarah asked:

"Do you… miss it? We could try to find…"

"No!" Lou interrupted. "I mean, it's where I was for most of my life. But… I don't think I was very happy there," Lou sounded really confused as she answered, and maybe a bit lost, too.

"Are there any people you miss?"

"No… the few people I cared for vanished."

Sarah blinked, that sounded ominous. For a moment she didn't know what to say, though she was incredibly curious about what kind of life Lou had led. Before she could start asking questions there came a loud meow from the cat and it looked at them, clearly displeased. Sarah took the hint and soon they settled down to sleep.

Confronting the past

There had been a big discussion between them regarding the search. Tanya, of course, had wanted to continue searching. Luka had pointed out that there wasn't much they could do at that moment since there was no magical trace to follow. He had also reminded her that they needed sleep. After some arguing, they had found and checked into a bed and breakfast. Luka had been against it, but Tanya had wanted to be close to where Sera had last been, and not having to bother with magical transportation was a plus. Luka had eventually given in.

There was one thing though she hadn't thought of and that was how awkward it would be to share a rather small space with her cousin. Which was where they were now, in two beds that were maybe a metre away from one another and oppressing silence around them. They were both lying in their respective beds, neither being able to sleep due to said silence. A few times one of them opened their mouths to speak but closed it again. This went on for a while until Tanya sighed and sat up in her bed, looking over at Luka.

"I reckon there is a lot we need to talk about."

Luka shifted a bit and sat up as well.

"Yes, there is…" Luka seemed unwilling to continue.

The silence stretched on, until Tanya gathered her courage:

"I suppose I could have handled things differently than I did."

"You mean other than accusing me of giving up on my family and trying to be someone I'm not?" Luka scoffed.

Tanya cringed. It sounded really bad put like that, and Luka sounding hurt made her feel worse.

"My mother was murdered, and you wanted to run off and live in a cave, rather than defend property that belonged to our ancestors!" she said.

She still remembered that day. She'd been living in her new house for a few months when there'd been a knock on the door. She'd opened it to find two guardians standing there. They'd had serious looks on their faces and she had tensed up, expecting to be accused of something to do with her magic. Instead, they had told her that her mother and aunt had been found dead far from their home, seemingly collecting herbs judging by the baskets found next to them. The guardians had suspected murder.

After that Tanya had hurried to her childhood home, and her cousin. Luka had tearfully confirmed it, explaining that they had gone on one of their exploration trips, something they did often after she and Luka had reached their late teens. Tanya had broken down at the news. She'd just felt empty. The days leading up to the funeral as well as the funeral itself were still hazy and she didn't recall much, though she had had a hand in it all, somehow. It wasn't until after the funeral that she had gathered herself somewhat as her cousin had informed her of his plans to leave for the mountains.

Said cousin's voice broke her out of her memories.

"My mother was murdered, too! And it's not like you were particularly eager to defend it either. Why was it my job, anyway?"

"You're the oldest, and it was left for you."

"Oh, is that what this is about? Because if you want it, you can have it."

"I don't want it. I already have a home. I just…" Tanya sighed, not knowing how to explain properly.

There was a banging on the door, a gruff voice shouting at them to shut up as people were trying to sleep.

She didn't know when they had moved to the foot of their beds, but now they were sitting almost nose to nose and glaring at each other. There was a banging on the wall as another guest also wanted them to shut up. Tanya deflated and glanced at the small clock on the nightstand. It was three in the morning. Now she just she felt drained and sad, earlier annoyance having vanished as the memories hit her.

"I'm sorry. Aunt Yana was just always so proud of the property and how we'd managed for generations to keep it to ourselves. You always seemed so keen on it too, you always spoke about making a few practical changes. I guess I just assumed you wanted it. And when you didn't, I just got so… mad." She could feel her eyes filling up as she spoke and was glad, she was staring at the floor rather than her cousin.

She heard Luka sigh.

"I wanted to run away, not from the house but from the memories. It didn't help that I was afraid the people who killed them would come after me. I was a mess, basically, and I know I said some horrible things to you as well, so I'm hardly innocent in this. I'm… sorry." The last word was mumbled.

Tanya looked at her cousin, who was now staring at the mattress he was sitting on. She could still remember his harsh words, about how she was self-absorbed and cared more about her herb collection than their mothers being dead.

That fight had been the worst they'd ever had. A lot of words had been said, or rather screamed. There had been some spells thrown as well, the anger making the two of them lose control of their magic. Thankfully, their aims had been off, and no one had been hit. The fight had ended with Luka storming off to his room and she had stood there fuming for a while before abruptly leaving the house to go back to her own place. It had taken a while for her to calm down enough to start missing her cousin and regret what had been said. But she hadn't heard anything from him in that time and was too scared, not to mention proud and stubborn, to reach out herself. The only communication she got from her old hometown after that was through the unofficial newsletter the local gossips insisted on sending to her, which was how she found out what Luka was doing for a living.

"I'm sorry too," she said.

Luka looked at her and gave her a tentative smile, which she returned. They lay back in their respective beds, both feeling lighter. Falling asleep was relatively easy after that.

New, worrying leads

(Day 3)

They woke up late in the morning, barely managing to get some breakfast before it stopped being served. Then they went back to the scene of the crime.

Standing in the alley Tanya felt like ripping her hair out. She was gripping it at the moment. There were no leads, and neither she nor Luka knew how to proceed. Luka was staring intently at the locket that had started this whole mess, like that could give him answers. Tanya was staring at the bins where the locket had been. There were no clues to be found.

"Should we... hire a detective?" Tanya asked slowly.

"Maybe we could hack into the security cameras," Luka suggested, pointing at a dirty camera in a corner.

"Do you know how to do that?" Tanya asked, curious.

"Um..." was Luka's response.

Tanya sighed, then groaned in frustration: "There has to be something we can do."

Luka's answer was slow:

"Well, there is this spell..."

"Yes?" she waited for him to continue.

"It can allow us to see what happened here, a look into the past so to speak. But it is complicated, and it takes a lot of energy," he trailed off, biting his lip.

"Well, let's do that then," she said. If nothing else, it might give them some clues.

"Like I said, it takes a lot of energy and…"

"And what?" She started to feel rather impatient and his trailing off didn't help.

"Well… what if someone sees us?"

Tanya looked pointedly around the alley and looked back at her cousin; eyebrow raised: "Do you think the people coming to this alley are the respectable, magic-fearing kind?"

Luka looked sheepish at that, then he took her hands in his: "Right, follow my lead."

Chanting together with someone was difficult, especially as neither of them had done that for a long time and it didn't help that the words were unfamiliar to Tanya. But she could feel the magic take effect, and soon a scene played out before them.

It was a worrying scene, the two men closing in on her girl looked like bad news. Tanya felt her breathing and heartbeat quicken. As the men grabbed Sera and the scene froze there was only one thought in her mind:

I have to find her!

"Whoa, that is really cool, man."

Tanya and Luka both flinched at the unexpected voice and turned as one towards the source. They came face to face with a young, unkempt man. He was walking wobbly, his eyes were reddish with big pupils and there was a sickly-sweet smell hanging about him. There was an odd smile on his face which made Tanya uncomfortable. He was also blocking the exit to the alley.

"You're looking for that little girl?" said the man pointing at the frozen image of Sera.

"Yes." Luka made a gesture with his hand and the image disappeared.

A tenseness Tanya hadn't been aware of released her as the spell was cancelled.

"Well, she's probably sold by now," the man said, matter-of-factly.

"What?" Tanya shrieked.

"Those men are part of Vicious Wilhelm's gang; they are notorious for kidnapping people. Everyone knows they're a bunch of slave traders."

Tanya's mind went blank, and her knees buckled. Luka grabbed hold of her and asked in a slightly shaky voice: "Do you, perhaps, know where the slave traders are?"

The man shrugged: "Rumour has it they usually do their business in the desert."

"Right... Thank you. We need to continue now," Luka said.

The man moved, letting them pass, and Luka dragged Tanya with him.

"Well, I guess we should ask around," Luka said, swallowing nervously.

                                  *

Somehow, they had acquired a guide. As they had asked around in a pub, they had found out some things. It had turned out there were a few other people gathered there who were looking for their loved ones that had recently been taken by the gang. And so there had been a group of them setting out into the desert, a man familiar with the desert leading them.

Having a guide was of course a good thing, and Tanya was grateful. But the feeling of gratefulness was hard to keep up as the man couldn't stop boasting about his tracking skills. Considering the tracks they were following were rather obvious footprints in the sand Tanya wasn't terribly impressed.

They had been walking for about an hour when they stopped, staring with wide eyes at the group of women that were walking towards them. A woman from their group let out a joyful scream and rushed forward, embracing one of the women from the other group. A few other exclamations were heard and more embracing. Tanya wasn't sure what was going on at first, until it clicked. She looked at the other group, hoping to see Sera. But her heart sank as there was no sign of her.

Everyone from their group was carrying bags with supplies, a lot of water bottles and some food, amongst other things. These were now distributed to the other group, who drank greedily. They were by now all sitting on the ground. Tanya was anxious to ask the other group about her apprentice, but knew they needed some time to gather their thoughts.

One of the women started talking, explaining how they had escaped their captors by storming out of the cages in a group, managing to tie up the captors and then leaving them there. They had walked for a while, getting away from their prison and then lay down to rest as night had fallen. Then, early that morning they had continued walking, wanting to get out of the desert. They had followed the footprints and had now run into them, which they were glad of, considering none of them had had much by way of supplies.

As the woman's story ended Tanya saw her chance.

"Did you… was there a young girl with you at some point?"

Another woman spoke up: "There were two little girls in my cage. One who had been there for days and another, slightly older, who was thrown in there shortly before we made our escape. They both ran off towards the forest as we stormed out."

"Forest?" Tanya asked.

The guide spoke up: "At the edge of the desert is a forest, called Sweet Blossom Forest. It's vast. It's not an easy place to find your way in. If your daughter is in there, then…" He trailed off, giving Tanya a compassionate look.

Tanya was determined not to lose hope.

"How do you know she went into the forest? Maybe she continued through the desert."

Another woman spoke up, shaking her head: "They didn't go this way, and any other way eventually leads to that forest. If it was me, I'd go in there, if for no other reason than because it's cooler and there's likely to be water in there."

Tanya nodded slowly, then she looked at the guide: "Can you take us there? Only to the edge, you don't need to go into it with us."

The guide bit his lip, hesitant. A woman from the group Tanya was in, spoke: "We need to head in that direction anyway, to pick up the culprits. Hopefully, they're still tied up where you lot left them."

Tanya looked at her, she, along with a few others, were wearing civilian clothing, but she spotted a badge inside the woman's jacket. They were guardians.

Tanya nodded and soon they were on their way.

*

It had taken a few hours to reach where the women had been kept. It certainly was a sight to behold; smashed wood all over the place, what looked like a makeshift stage torn apart, and men strewn about the ground. The women had done a good job with the bindings for it to last that long, only two of the men had managed to loosen the ropes around their wrists. The guardians had quickly subdued the men and called for transport. Then the guardian in charge pointed Tanya and Luka in the right direction of the forest, opting to go back to the town with the other guardians.

It took a while to get there, an hour at least. Seeing a forest bordering a desert felt quite unreal. The cousins shared a look, then they each took a drink of water, squared their shoulders and stepped forward to enter the forest.

"Not so fast!"

A strong gust of wind pushed them backwards, landing on their backsides and they found themselves staring at what looked like a big cloud of smoke with glowing, orange eyes.

"Uh…" Tanya was unsure what to say.

"This forest is off limits to humas," the smoke creature hissed, its mouth just looking like a black hole in the middle of its body.

"Right," Tanya slowly got to her feet and pulled Luka up as well. "We're looking for someone and last we heard she was in this forest."

"Oh indeed? Yes, there were two little humans that slipped in here the other day, just when I was on my lunch break. Pesky, sneaky, awful humans! And they call us monsters. Can't someone have their lunch in peace without you lot trespassing, huh? What's wrong with you?" the creature snarled, the bottom of its body turning a glowing orange shade.

That was when Tanya realised the creature was almost as big as her and seemed to be growing, which was slightly unsettling. Never mind that she had never heard of anything like it before.

"What do you even eat? Aren't you made of smoke?" Luka asked, head tilted in curiosity.

Tanya elbowed him in the ribs just as the creature suddenly flew at them, now looking to be made half of flames and half smoke. The two of them stumbled back.

"Get lost!" Its voice rumbled like thunder.

"Okay, look," Tanya held up her hands in a calming way. "Since you hate people being in the forest so much, how about you let us go in there to get the children out?"

The creature grinned, an unpleasant sight that made Tanya back up a step by pure instinct.

"Oh, I don't think that's a problem anymore. They're most certainly dead by now. The dwellers of the forest will have made sure of it."

Tanya felt her heart drop to her feet as she stared at the creature in horror. The creature dropped the grin and snarled something at them, but she couldn't hear it as her ears were suddenly full of a ringing sound. There was a hand on her shoulder and the rumble of Luka's voice, which she couldn't hear clearly either. The creature's mouth moved again and Luka's grip on her shoulder tightened.

There was a tugging sensation in her stomach as Luka transported them away. As soon as they landed Tanya sank to the floor, completely heartbroken.

The more the merrier

(Day 4)

Sarah had always been fond of plants. It was just something about them that drew her to them. Before coming into Tanya's care, she had spent a lot of time out and about amongst plants, enjoying the sight and scents of them. Of all the theory she was learning from Tanya she enjoyed the plant lessons the most. And it was because of that knowledge she had managed to find enough plants in the forest to make a meal.

They had found a spring with fresh water, Lou had made a fire, and soon the water was boiling with a bunch of the plants thrown in. Not the tastiest soup perhaps, but it was warm and would give them energy to keep going. The cat had gone off to hunt for its own food.

It was the first time Sarah had had any use of the tin bowl in her pouch.

Sarah covered her hands with the bottom of her shirt and grabbed the hot bowl. She put it down on the ground to let it cool a bit before they ate it. In the meantime, they had some mushed berries to tide them over.

Suddenly there was a commotion and three figures tumbled out of a set of thick bushes, followed by an angrily hissing familiar. The girls stared open-mouthed at these figures who appeared to be arguing. Then one of them, who was clearly a gnome, detangled herself from the pile they were in and looked at the girls:

"Well, isn't this a surprise. Not often one sees humans 'round these parts," she said.

Sarah wasn't sure how to respond to that. But before she could try one of the other figures who looked like a troll walked up to her, stood in her personal space and... sniffed her?

"Hey!" she scooted away, glaring.

"Well, well, as I live and breathe. A magic user!"

Sarah wasn't sure if the exclamation was a good thing, and that combined with the way Lou was staring at her with wide eyes made her want to flee. But before she could even get to her feet the third figure spoke:

"Please excuse my siblings, they are being quite rude," was said pointedly towards the other two. "I'm Ekk and this is Fin and Tav," he continued, gesturing towards the troll and gnome, respectively.

"Um... siblings?" she couldn't help but ask, bewildered.

"Half-siblings, Ekk and I are siblings and he and Fin are as well, but I am in no way related to Fin," Tav clarified in a firm tone.

Sarah nodded as if she understood, it did explain why Ekk looked so... odd if he was half gnome and half troll.

Before she could think more about it there was a mewling sound from the cat.

"Oh! And he wants you to know that his name is Mr Wilkins," Ekk informed them.

"Right," Sarah nodded slowly, before remembering her manners: "I'm Sarah."

"I'm Lou," Lou said quietly.

"We happened to smell your cooking as we were walking along. It smells really good," Ekk said with a hopeful look on his face.

Sarah felt compelled to offer: "If you would like to taste…"

She hadn't even finished the sentence when Fin basically dove into the bowl. Before she knew it, the soup was all gone and Fin was wiping his mouth with the back of his hand, looking very satisfied. With an annoyed sigh she gathered more water from the spring and took out more plants from her pouch. Then she saw that Ekk and Tav were holding out their own bowls. They were smaller than hers and made of stone rather than tin. It was a relief because her own bowl was barely large enough for two portions. After filling their bowls, she put all of them on the fire, and soon enough it was bubbling away. She glanced at them, wondering where they had kept their bowls but decided against asking. Next, she glanced at the cat who had curled up beside her:

"Mr Wilkins?" she grinned slightly.

Mr Wilkins glanced at her with one eye as if daring her to make fun of his name and she laughed quietly.

The soup was finished and eaten mostly in silence. Sarah and Lou shared, and to Sarah's surprise Lou didn't act any differently towards her. She didn't shy away from Sarah in any case, but Sarah thought it might be best to keep her distance.

"So, where are you girls headed?" Tav asked, breaking the silence.

"Towards civilisation, Mr Wilkins is leading us," Sarah answered.

"Well, we're heading in the same direction. Our acting troupe is close to where you are going. How about we go together?" Ekk suggested.

Acting troupe? Sarah thought, baffled. She nodded in response.

*

They were an odd collection of beings walking along, led by a cat. Sarah and Lou were silently taking up the rear, while the other three were chatting merrily between themselves.

Lou was walking slightly in front of Sarah when she suddenly and quietly spoke up: "Are you really a magic user?"

Sarah flinched; she had been dreading this moment:

"Yes," she answered slowly.

Lou spoke quietly and slowly, hesitantly, but clearly curious:

"So, you can cast spells and stuff."

"Sort of…"

"Why haven't you?"

"My powers don't work right now."

"Why not?"

"Don't know."

"If they worked, could you get us other kinds of food?"

"I don't think so. I've only recently started getting lessons."

"Can you read?"

That was unexpected, and Sarah had to shake herself to readjust to the conversation:

"Well… yes."

"That's so cool. I wish I could read."

"Yeah… it's a good thing to know."

"What kind of stories do you read?"

"Well, I like adventure books." Honestly, she read very little besides the books Tanya assigned to her, and right now she felt a bit guilty about that.

"There was this woman on the ship who read to me when I was very little. They were mostly fairy stories. I really liked those… but the magic users in there were always old, evil and ugly," Lou gave Sarah a questioning look.

"Um… yeah, that's usually how the stories tell it. But that's far from the truth. My mentor, for instance, is young, talented and very kind. Some of her older friends are maybe a bit moody and not exactly beautiful. But I've never met anyone I'd call evil."

"What's a mentor?"

"Well, um… She takes care of me and she's teaching me magic and other skills I might need."

"So, she's like your mother?"

"Well, no…um…. huh," Sarah stared emptily ahead as those words hit her. Was Tanya her mum?

Lou gave her an odd look and she realised how weird that must have sounded. But before she could try to come up with an explanation Lou said: "Tell me about her?"

Sarah smiled and started talking.

*

They had been talking a lot. They had covered a lot of ground as well and rushing water could be heard nearby. Sarah had found out things about Lou too in exchange for information about her own life with Tanya. A lot of what she had found out was not very pleasant, Lou had certainly not led an easy life. From the sound of it Lou had lived on an honest to goodness pirate ship. She had been used as labour since she could keep hold of a mop and most of the chores on the ship had been designated to her. She had been treated poorly by most of the ship's crew and rarely talked because of the risk of being yelled at. If someone had taken interest in her and taken her under their wing they disappeared sooner or later, though the reason for that wasn't all that clear. Why she had been given to the slave traders was a mystery, and Sarah was relieved that they had managed to escape together. She had unexpectedly become very protective of Lou and was determined to make sure Lou would get a happy life from now on.

By this point they had been walking for a long time and it was dark. She wasn't sure of the time, but she suspected it was around midnight or later. Suddenly everyone stopped and stared. Fin made a shushing gesture and crouched down behind a tree trunk, gesturing for them to do the same. Sarah and Lou hid together. Sarah peeked around the trunk, squinting in the gloom to see what had spooked the others.

Oh dear, she thought to herself.

Hope

Luka managed to get her off the floor and into a chair. Soon there was a steaming cup of tea in her hands which turned out to be incredibly sweet. The sweetness helped her come out of her trance and she looked down at her cousin who was crouching in front of her, feeling completely lost as to what to do next.

"Tanya… I wouldn't take what that… thing said to heart. There is still every chance that Sera is alive."

"I guess," she looked down at her tea.

After a moment of silence Luka spoke up, his tone hesitant.

"If you want… we could ask the cards or the tea leaves for a sign, to know if she's… alive."

Tanya swallowed, her throat feeling tight all of a sudden.

"Yeah, that's probably a good idea." Her voice shook as she spoke.

Luka nodded, got to his feet and walked away. Tanya finished her tea and closed her eyes, trying to calm her breathing and keep her thoughts on Sera before turning the cup three times in her hands. She had just turned the cup upside down on the saucer when Luka returned. He was holding a deck of cards in one hand and dice in the other.

"I thought, best out of three...?" he spoke slowly in response to her raised eyebrow.

She nodded and set the teacup and saucer on the table.

Seeing Luka shuffle the cards and rolling the dice gave her an idea as to why people kept coming to him for his little magic/fortune-telling shows. She kept her eyes on his hands even as he'd finished, and everything was set on the table. Luka met her eyes, she nodded, and they clasped hands. Together they looked down.

"Well, I'd say that's a good sign," Luka commented.

"Yeah..." Tanya answered.

While the cards were uncertain the tea leaves and the dice gave positive signs. Tanya clasped her necklace and let herself hope.

*

It wasn't until they were eating dinner that Tanya spoke again. Luka had kept up some idle, non-important chatter as they prepared the food.

"Thank you, Luka. You have done so much for me these past few days and gone above and beyond. You didn't need to, but you did, and for that you have my sincere thanks."

Luka blinked at her, looking bemused and strangely hurt by her words.

"Of course, I'll help. You're family, both you and Sera.

"Yeah… look, I think I need to go. I've taken up far too much of your time already, I'm sure you have better things to do and…"

"No."

"What do you mean no?"

Luka stood up from his chair and went to stand in front of her, arms crossed and frowning.

"I mean no, you're not leaving. Or if you are I'll simply follow you home. Point is, I'm not letting you go through this alone."

"Luka…"

"Tanya."

The two of them stared at each other, each as stubborn as the other. But Tanya recognised the look on her cousin's face and knew she couldn't win this. And in all honesty, she didn't want to.

"Fine. I'll stay. Thank you."

*

They were sitting in the living room. Tanya could feel despair slowly setting in as Luka spoke up.

"I hope you don't mind me asking, but I'm incredibly curious about this. What made you take Sera in?"

Tanya smiled at the memory:

"Well, I was in the woods close to my house picking herbs when this little girl comes up to me. Children, and adults even, rarely come that close to the woods so I was a bit surprised. She started asking me about the herbs and I answered her. Then, out of nowhere, she grabbed some of my herbs and started eating them. When I got over the shock, I gave her a peach I had on me and told her to go home before I left. But I continued seeing her in and around the woods and by the village. Then a storm was approaching, and I saw her close to my house in a grassy field. She continued just sitting there in the field when the rain started falling, and when it started really pouring, I'd had enough and went over there to drag her inside. It was just in time before the first clap of thunder came. I scolded her and told her about the dangers of sitting in a field during a storm, particularly if there was lightning. Then she stayed with me for three days until the storm stopped. During those three days I accidentally revealed my magic, and she showed me hers in return. After that I managed to figure out where she came from and took her there, a sanctuary in a town two hours away. Once I came back home I… well, I felt a bit lonely as her company had been nice. And a few hours later she was there again, knocking on my door. She kept coming back no matter how many times I returned her there, and eventually both I and the matron in charge of the sanctuary grew tired of it. So, after a long conversation between the three of us I was her guardian and mentor. And that's how it happened."

The small smile on Luka's face matched her own.

"Did it seem like a good sanctuary?" he asked softly.

Tanya nodded.

"Yes, the matron cared very much for the children. She had even managed, somehow, to get some funding for it. Even so, their resources were limited and just caring for them took so much time that there was barely any time left for education. Sera always had so many questions when she showed up at my place. I realised I liked teaching her, which was part of why I decided to make her my apprentice" Tanya smiled. Yes, her apprentice liked to learn, but her interest was limited and trying to teach her about things outside her interests was a trial.

Luka smiled, reassured. Then they both decided it was time for bed.

Getting closer

It was a wolgan, a wolf-like creature with scales that went from the top of its head, down its back and all the way down to its tail which tip looked somewhat like a fin. There was also a river with a bridge to cross over, which the wolgan was blocking. And it didn't look friendly.

"I completely forgot! I don't have an offering," Tav whispered frantically.

"M…Maybe we have something, I'll check," Ekk muttered.

With that he took off a backpack Sarah hadn't noticed before, it blended perfectly into the waistcoat he was wearing. Then what they had said registered:

"Offering?"

"To cross over the bridge, you need to give it something," Tav said as she and the other two looked through the backpack.

"Speaking of which, do you have anything?" Fin asked.

"I… um, I have some coin," she said uncertainly.

"Silly mortal," the new voice made them all jump: "What use would I have of coin?"

The wolgan was standing about two metres away from them, staring at them judgementally. Sarah stared at it, scared and fascinated. But she felt rather surprised:

"You can talk?"

"Of course!" the wolgan sounded offended.

"But there are no records of wolgans being able to talk," she didn't mean to sound so accusing.

The wolgan scoffed:

"Records. You mean that humans write? Why would we want to talk to humans?"

"Right… fair enough," then she remembered what the wolgan had said at first and she blurted: "You know you're a mortal too."

The wolgan's eyes narrowed, and someone whimpered. Sarah's mouth seemed to have a life of its own as she continued.

"Besides, why do we have do give you something to cross? Is it your bridge, did you build it?"

The wolgan's glowing green eyes had grown wider and wider as she spoke, and Sarah noticed in her peripheral vision that Lou and Mr Wilkins were standing slightly behind her, the cat looked oddly smug, while the other three had backed some distance away.

"You have a clever tongue little one, maybe I should rip it out of your mouth," it said, eyes still wide but its tone was a mix of angry and arrogant.

The glowing eyes that were fixed on her felt more unnerving than the words it had uttered. But it didn't move, which felt slightly reassuring. And Sarah was tired, again it struck her how late it must be. She sighed heavily:

"Can we continue this conversation tomorrow? I'm exhausted."

And with that she lay down on the ground and fell asleep.

*

(Day 5)

She awoke to laughter. It took a while to remember where she was. When she did, she felt cold inside. Had she really spoken that way to a wolgan of all creatures, one that could kill everyone without breaking a sweat?

Before she could start panicking, she realised that the laughter was the relaxed kind, as in, not coming from a satisfied creature that had just performed an evil deed. She sat up slowly, feeling sore from lying on the ground. Rubbing her face she saw that Lou was sitting close by, attention on the rest of their small group a few metres away by a fire. Though she noticed that the group had grown bigger as the wolgan was there too, and it was smiling and laughing with the others.

"What's going on?" she asked Lou quietly.

Lou startled but smiled slightly as she turned to her. "Turns out you're the only one who's ever spoken to Val like that before. It surprised her. You were right, it's not exactly her bridge, she was guarding it because the ones who built it partially destroyed her home, and she didn't want to risk it being destroyed any more. Everyone just assumed she wanted payment so they could cross, and she got used that."

"Huh, so… In a way it is her bridge," Sera mused, distantly noting this was the first time she'd heard Lou speak that many sentences at once.

"I suppose. Anyway, she and Mr Wilkins talked for a while, and then they went to hunt together. They're cooking it now over the fire, there's enough for all of us."

Sarah licked her lips as the smell of cooked meat reached her. She smiled at Lou, and they went over to the others.

"Ah, there's our sleeping beauty," Fin said as she and Lou sat down.

Sarah glared slightly at him and then offered Val a smile who smiled back. They ate and talked. It all felt very cheerful and relaxed. As the others talked Sarah leaned towards Lou.

"Were you awake all night?"

"Not all night, I fell asleep a while after you and woke up when Val and Mr Wilkins went to hunt together."

"Right."

As the meal finished the atmosphere grew a bit sombre. The group knew they should leave but they didn't want to leave Val, and she didn't want to be left alone. She felt like a friend, even after such a short time, and it was clear that she was lonely.

"You know," Val said slowly; "I have been meaning to see some more of this forest, and maybe the rest of the world. I have been too stuck in my ways to start, but maybe…"

"You want to come with us?!" Tav exclaimed, delighted.

"If you don't mind…" Val's tail started wagging.

"Of course we don't mind. And hey, maybe you'll take a fancy to acting," Ekk grinned.

Fin just shrugged as if he couldn't care less, but as he turned away there was a gentle smile on his face. Even Mr Wilkins looked pleased, as pleased as a cat could look, and Sarah and Lou gave supportive smiles and thumbs up.

They helped Val pack her belongings, there weren't many, and soon they were on their way.

*

It was sometime around dinner time, judging by the sun, as Mr Wilkins stopped abruptly. He turned towards them and nodded to Lou and Sarah.

"Well, it seems this is where we must part. It's not too far of a walk for you three to get out of the forest to civilisation. Mr Wilkins will lead you. And we're going another way to our fellow actors," Ekk explained, looking a bit sad.

Sarah felt a bit sad too. On the one hand she really looked forward to getting out of the forest and, somehow, getting back to Tanya. But on the other hand, she didn't like the thought of never seeing these four again. They felt like friends, and she had grown fond of them.

"I'll miss you. You have been terribly kind to two lost girls. And I'm so grateful," she smiled sadly as she spoke.

"We'll miss you, too. But maybe we'll see each other again someday," Tav said with a hopeful smile on her face.

"I'd like that," Sarah said.

They hugged. It took a while to hug everyone, and she might have taken a bit longer than necessary to not leave straight away. Mr Wilkins made a grumbling sound.

"You take care now. Take care of each other," Fin told them sternly as everyone had finished hugging.

"You too, and good luck with the acting," Sarah grinned.

They waved as they left. Mr Wilkins led them.

Communications

(Day 4)

Tanya woke early in the morning, and it took a while to remember where she was and why she was there. As she did, she started to feel restless. It was too early in the morning to start enacting the plan she had come up with before going to sleep, but she felt too jittery to try falling back to sleep. After staring up at the ceiling for a while she decided to get up.

Without thinking about it her feet took her to the family room, and her heart ached at the sight. This was a room where she had spent many happy hours. Even after her uncle's disappearance they had still had fun in here. And now it was ruined, probably during a grief-induced rage on Luka's part. Goodness knew she had had some of those herself.

Staring at the mess she felt determination rise in her chest, and she started cleaning. Opening the window, she chucked everything broken out on the lawn. She let the sofa be as the hole, though large, was fixable. It could do with a touch up anyway, in the form of new upholstering. Then she considered the wallpaper. As it was pretty much shredded there seemed to be no point in trying to save it. And with that thought she started tearing it off. It was weirdly cathartic. She couldn't help but grin softly as she finished, considering the floor was messier than before. With an amused huff, she summoned a bag she had seen in the kitchen earlier and shoved the mess in there. Then she gasped as she noticed the time.

She rushed down to the kitchen and started making breakfast. She still felt like she needed to thank Luka somehow so making a special breakfast seemed like a good idea. Luckily, the ingredients she needed were either in the kitchen or in her pouch. Soon, a wonderful smell started spreading through the house.

Just as she finished Luka came into the kitchen, an awed look on his face. As he took in the contents of the plates on the table he smiled hugely.

As they sat down to eat Luka said, "Did you know fairies enjoy the smell of the honey-scented soap and shampoo you make?"

Tanya looked at him in surprise.

"You've tried my products?"

Luka blushed.

"Yes, well… yes."

Tanya smiled a bit at that, then frowned in confusion.

"I don't remember any orders sent to this address."

"I've rented a box at the post office."

"I see… And how did you figure out fairies like it?" Tanya asked with a laugh.

"I spent some time close to a nest, studying a fungus I had found. It wasn't information I was searching for, but I happened to get it anyway. The fairies uh… They tried to eat my hair," Luka muttered, running his fingers through his hair, eyes on his food.

Tanya sputtered a laugh, more out of surprise than amusement. It felt nice to laugh though, it felt like ages since she'd last done it. Then she smiled a bit wistfully.

"You always were the more studious of the two of us," she mumbled. "Maybe I should have you teach Sera instead."

"Speaking of your daughter, I have an idea of how we can proceed with the search," Luka's tone changed drastically, as he was clearly eager to change the subject. Tanya twitched a bit at the word daughter, but she perked up as he finished the sentence.

"So have I," she grinned.

"Contacting other witches," they both said simultaneously.

Grinning at each other they finished their food. Then Tanya stood up and clapped her hands together, ready for action.

"Right, where's your mirror?"

Luka blinked at her.

"We can send out messages using my raven," he countered.

Tanya put her hands on her hips and gave her cousin an incredulous look.

"Do you know how long that would take? A mirror is more effective. Now come on, where do you keep it?"

Luka just looked at her strangely as a large raven landed on his shoulder,

Where did that come from? Tanya thought and flinched as it turned towards her. Its beak looked sharp.

"Tanya, meet Francis. He'll be happy to carry messages, he can take several at once."

The raven, Francis apparently, nodded in agreement.

"Hello Francis," Tanya said politely. "I don't mean to be rude, but it'll take far too long for you to deliver all those messages, and even longer to wait for responses, especially compared to how quick a mirror is," she explained, hoping she wouldn't offend him.

Francis gave Luka a look as if to say I told you so, and then he flew off. Luka sighed and scratched the back of his head. Tanya gaped at him as she understood.

"You don't have a mirror?"

"I have a mirror, a normal one to see my reflection in, not to use as a communication device," Luka said defensively, pouting slightly.

"You can use it for both, communicating through it does not make it so you can't see your reflection," Tanya informed him impatiently, rolling her eyes.

With that she started walking towards the bathroom.

"Performing the communication spell is a bit tricky, but it shouldn't take too long," she said as she walked.

Luka grabbed her shoulder and spun her around. He looked almost… frightened.

"But it's not safe," he insisted.

"What do you mean?" she asked, confused.

"Someone could track you with it," he shivered slightly as he spoke.

"Luka… While that is possible that is not going to happen," she tried to reassure him.

"How could you possibly know that?" Luka demanded.

"Because! I just know. Okay? I trust my fellow witches not to betray me like that."

Luka did not look entirely reassured, but he conceded with the words.

"The mirror in the attic is better, hang on a moment and I will fetch it."

It was a big, oval mirror with a golden frame engraved with circular patterns. They had hung it in a corner of the living room, where Luka kept a small table full of knick-knacks for his little magic shows, as well as a chair. Tanya had performed the spell; it had taken longer than she would have liked but when it came to a spell like this one, she had to make sure to get it right.

She was now sitting on the chair and four faces were staring at her from the mirror, five with her own and six if one counted Luka's curious but wary face behind hers.

"Why, hello handsome," the oldest of them grinned at Luka.

Luka flinched a bit and Tanya sighed, a sound which was echoed by one of the other faces.

"Helga."

Helga stopped grinning and looked at the one who had sighed her name.

"Yes, Myrna?"

Myrna glared and opened her mouth to start arguing with her aunt, but another voice spoke up.

"Why have you called us, Tanya?" Out of all of them Lily was probably the most sensible one. She was around the same age as Tanya.

All the faces looked at Tanya. Tanya swallowed.

"I am rather in need of some help."

"Help with what?" The second eldest, Carmen, asked.

"My apprentice has gone missing. I would like some help to keep an eye out for her."

"She was last seen entering the Sweet Blossom Forest with another little girl," Luka explained.

All eyes turned to him. Tanya put a hand on his shoulder in support as he clearly was uncomfortable with the attention.

"Who is this fine-looking young man, Tanya? I didn't know you were married," Helga exclaimed, giving Tanya an accusing stare.

Tanya rolled her eyes.

"I'm not. This is my cousin who believes that revealing his name will get his soul stolen."

Luka elbowed her with an annoyed look.

"It's not his soul I'm interested in," Helga said with a wicked smile.

Luka cringed. Tanya and the others groaned.

"You're a stereotype Helga, and not just a witchy one," Tanya informed her.

Everyone politely avoided looking at the rather large wart on Helga's nose at those words. Helga just gave a shrill cackling laugh in response as if to confirm those words. All of them winced at that.

"Honestly," Myrna muttered.

Immediately aunt and niece started bickering. Tanya slammed her hands on top of the table in front of the mirror.

"If we could get back to business," she said as all eyes focused on her.

As everyone turned towards her and kept quiet, she continued, "Now, I'm not expecting anyone to enter the forest, I am only asking you to keep an eye and a feel out for her. As my cousin said, there might be another little girl with her, and we don't know what she looks like. But my apprentice looks like this." She held up the photograph she kept in her pouch.

The rest of them nodded seriously.

"Don't worry Tanya, we'll keep our eyes open. And I, for one, will contact a few others I know who live near that forest and ask them to do the same," Lily assured her.

The others concurred and promised to do likewise. Tanya thanked them all sincerely and the call ended. She sat down on a nearby chair with a half-sigh and a half-groan.

"Now what?" she asked.

"Now, we wait," Luka patted her shoulder.

Great, she thought sarcastically.

Distractions

(Day 5)

She hated waiting, especially in a situation like this. Sera was in a dangerous forest full of dangerous creatures, and there was nothing she could do about it. She hated it.

She had woken up early again and was contemplating the family room to distract herself. But her thoughts went to Sera. Luka was sitting on the sofa, his head leaning against his hand and dozing lightly.

"Hey," Tanya said.

"Wh… what?" Luka grunted, sitting up.

"What was that smoke thingy by the forest?"

"I'm not sure, I've never seen anything like it before," Luka muttered, rubbing the sleep from his eyes.

"I see… Couldn't we have entered the forest somewhere else?"

"No. According to that one there were several of them guarding the forest. I didn't think it was worth the risk, and you were in shock or something, so I thought it was best to get you away from there."

"Oh, right."

She sat down on the sofa and stared emptily ahead. After a while she asked, "Sweet Blossom Forest has suppressor fields, right? Will they harm her?"

"I don't think so. People with magic have entered that forest before and come out just fine, magic-wise. At most she will be unable to cast any spells and she might feel more tired than usual."

"Good," Tanya sighed.

She had been in suppressor fields herself a few times. That feeling of her magic suddenly not working, of her magic seeming to have vanished, was extremely unpleasant and usually left her feeling shaken up and almost out of breath as long as she was in said field. The shaken-up feeling usually stayed a while after getting out of there. But she had only experienced them as an adult and was unsure of how they affected children.

She shook herself and decided to change the subject.

"So, do you think we should paint the walls or find some cheery wallpaper to put up?"

Luka stared at her incomprehensively for a moment before it seemed to click.

"I don't know," Luka groaned, "maybe we should just chuck out the sofa and let this room stand empty."

"What? You can't do that!" Tanya exclaimed, aghast.

"It's a family room, Tanya. There's no family here to use it,"

"Well, then I'll simply start visiting with Sera once she's found. We can have weekly… movie nights or something." She lifted her face slightly; a stubborn expression Luka was familiar with.

He huffed a laugh.

"Movie nights? Do you even know how a telly works?"

She squirmed.

"No, but I can't imagine it'll be hard to figure out. I know Sera would like it; she's mentioned being interested in a telly. Besides, it would be a good opportunity to expand… our cultural… range," she said haltingly.

Luka looked as if he was about to burst into laughter:

"I didn't know movies counted as culture."

She glared at him.

"That depends on what you're watching… Anyway, we don't have to make it to a movie room. We can have weekly game nights or something instead."

Luka's smile was gentler as she finished speaking.

"It's a good idea. We could make it into an entertainment room, with a telly and everything."

She smiled:

"Sounds good," then she bit her lip, uncertainly, "but costly…"

"Don't worry, I've got plenty," Luka said, rather flippantly in Tanya's opinion.

"Really?" she said with one eyebrow raised.

"Yes, well… My parlour games as you call them are quite successful. Putting on a good show in front of receptive people can make you a lot of money," Luka explained, "and I don't really spend much money on things, only necessities, so I've saved up a lot."

Tanya grinned slightly.

"I can believe that. You seemed quite skilled with both cards and the dice yesterday, though I have to admit it's hard to imagine you putting on a show in front of people when you've seemed so uncomfortable around the people we've interacted with these past few days."

Luka shrugged.

"When I'm performing, I'm the one in control, you know? Talking to people without any time to prepare is hard."

"You don't seem to have any trouble talking to me."

"Yes, well, that's because it's you."

Tanya blinked. She wasn't sure that made much sense, but she felt flattered anyway.

"I see… Anyway, I'm not letting you pay for everything. I have a bit saved up we can use too."

"Right, yes, good idea. How about we make some breakfast and get going?" he asked.

"It's still early."

"The earlier we're done the faster we can get everything else done," he gestured around the room.

"I suppose you're right." She gave him a mischievous grin. "Last one to the kitchen has to do the dishes." She sprinted off.

"Hey!" she heard him sprinting after her.

She yelped as she was suddenly lifted into the air and Luka ran past her, putting her down on the floor as soon as he'd passed.

"That's cheating!"

He was already in the kitchen and mixing up ingredients as she got there, giving her a smug grin as she entered the room.

"I was thinking about making pancakes and slathering them with syrup."

"I'm rather in the mood for some toast," she countered. "Also, I thought you didn't like syrup?"

He snorted.

"All right, you got me there. Pancakes with jam then."

She rolled her eyes and huffed but nodded. Since he was already mixing the ingredients there was no point in arguing further. She headed over to start setting the table, sticking out her tongue at him along the way and grinning as he laughed.

*

They had decided on painting the family room and headed to the shopping district. Finding a shop open early had been tricky but fortunately one shopkeeper had been an early riser and willing to part with a few cans of paint and other painting supplies for some extra coin. Once they had finished that purchase the other shops were starting to open so they had managed to get everything they needed fairly early. Luka had insisted on buying a new sofa as well.

Luckily, it was a magic-friendly shopping district, like the rest of the town, so they could just shrink the big stuff and put them in their bags. Then they had gone back and started painting the room a dark blue colour. That part they did by hand as they had both learned when they were younger that magic and home renovations didn't work out very well, though drying the paint with some magic help was perfectly acceptable. Then they had started setting everything up with some magical aid and finished in time for a late lunch.

As they finished eating, they went back to the room and ended up crouched down, staring at the telly.

"How does it work?" Tanya said slowly, mostly to herself.

"Good question," Luka mumbled beside her.

Tanya slowly raised her hand and put her thumb and middle finger together to snap them, but Luka grabbed her wrist:

"Don't!"

"Why?" she asked, confused.

"You know magic and technology don't work well together." He raised his eyebrows meaningfully.

"Right," she put her hand down, blushing at the reminder.

The scorch mark on the wall out in the hallway outside the room told part of the story of her earlier mishap with trying to mix the two together. There was a dent in the wall by the ceiling diagonally across from the scorch mark that told more of the story. Both had been preserved by her aunt and mother as a reminder to not be so reckless again. Looking at either gave her a phantom headache, which was why she avoided doing so.

"Anyway, how about you go take a shower and I'll have a go at this?" he suggested.

At her raised eyebrow he explained, "You have paint in your hair."

"Right," she mumbled, then turned towards the bathroom.

*

Getting the paint out of her hair had been a pain and had required half a shampoo bottle. While she was still very happy about the fact that Luka used her products, it was a shame in this case that he didn't own the shampoo she had developed just for getting nasty stuff out of one's hair. But she managed to get it out all the same and was absently making plans of replacing Luka's shampoo, and maybe get him some more products to try, as she got out of the shower. It was as she was drying off as Luka suddenly knocked on the door:

"Come on, hurry up! Seraphina just called."

"What?" she exclaimed.

Quickly tying the towel around herself she hurried out, slipping in the water dripping from her in the process. Fortunately, Luka caught her and got her upright, then he rolled his eyes at her and gestured with his hand at her which dried her instantly. She blushed at her own folly

before she gestured herself and her clothes were on her in
the next second. Luka grabbed her hand, and they were off.

Into the orchard

(Day 5)

They were finally out of the forest. Somehow the air here seemed much fresher. Sarah felt much more energetic, as if she had walked around in a half-asleep state the past few days without realising and just now woken up completely.

Admittedly, it was a bit hard to tell at first that they were outside the forest since they were still surrounded by trees. But on closer inspection these trees were quite a bit shorter than the ones in the forest and were rather neatly lined up in rows.

Suddenly Mr Wilkins sprinted away; the two girls exchanged a look and sprinted after him. They came to a fenced off area, which they could easily jump over. There they stopped and gaped.

"What are those?" Lou asked, bewildered.

"Blue teardrops," Sarah whispered, enraptured. "I've never actually seen them before, they're very rare."

She raised a hand to grab one from a low-hanging branch when, out of nowhere, a large hand slapped hers, hard. She wrenched her hand towards her chest as her magic reacted instinctively and pushed her attacker away from herself and Lou. In the back of her mind she felt relieved that her magic was working again, but her focus was on the attacker, an older lady who was giving them both a stern look. Mr Wilkins was standing about a metre behind her and appeared to be shaking his head at them.

"Has no one taught you not to touch things that don't belong to you?" the lady said sternly, hands on her hips.

Sarah cradled her sore hand and glared.

"I was following the cat, and I just wanted to look," it wasn't a good defence, but she didn't want to be lectured by a stranger.

The lady was now looking at them closely, slightly frowning.

"You don't live around here. Where did you come from?"

"The forest," Lou whispered in response when Sarah was too busy pouting to do so.

"Hm," the lady huffed, then ordered: "Come with me."

She turned around and started walking towards a house, Mr Wilkins followed, and they felt they had no other choice but to do so as well.

The inside of the house smelled deliciously of warm apples, sugar and cinnamon. The girls licked their lips and their stomachs growled loudly. The lady led them into a kitchen, where a younger woman and a small girl, about Lou's age, were busy sprinkling sugar on a few pies. The woman looked up and her eyebrows rose.

"Madame, did you bring dinner guests?"

"Yes, I found them in the special orchard. I think we should invite Evelyn as well, seeing as this one," she pointed at Sarah, "is magic."

Sarah stiffened, wondering if this Evelyn was a magic hunter. But she noticed Mr Wilkins nodding along with these words, and she couldn't detect any disgust on the strangers' faces as the lady said this, so she decided to wait and see. The offer of dinner certainly helped make up her mind.

Lou and she were directed to another room which held a big-ish table, along with the other girl who had introduced herself as Aki. They sat down and Aki started asking a lot of questions.

"Are you really a magic user? Which spells do you know? Where did you come from? Where are your parents? Do you know how to knit? Can you summon rain whenever you need it? Do you know any spell that keep apples fresh longer?"

As Aki paused for breath Sarah stared at her, smiling stiffly and not knowing how to respond at all. She glanced at Lou who was looking at Aki almost admiringly.

"Um…" She started, not knowing how to continue.

"Are those two women your mother and grandmother?" Lou spoke up.

Sarah sighed in relief as Aki was now looking at Lou instead.

"Yes, well, they're my mother and Madame Kimiko," Aki said, as if that explained everything.

"Right… And what use does this Madame Kimiko have of blue teardrops?" Sarah was pretty sure Madame Kimiko wasn't a magic user, so it didn't make sense.

"Oh, those are Evelyn's, a neighbour. She helps out with our orchard, and we give her a small plot of land in return, and make sure her plants are fed and watered."

"Oh," Sarah mumbled quietly.

Further conversation was interrupted by Madame Kimiko, Aki's mother and a third woman entering the room. Sarah and the woman both stiffened and regarded one another.

"You must be Evelyn," Sarah smiled, a little cautious, but relieved to see a fellow witch.

"And you're Seraphina," Evelyn smiled back.

Sarah flinched. She was sure she had not introduced herself to Madame Kimiko and Aki's mother, and if she had she would not have used that name. Out of the corner of her eye she could see Lou giving her a look she wasn't sure the meaning of. But before she could react further the women sat down, digging into the food they had brought with them and telling the girls to go ahead. Everyone eating postponed any further conversation.

When the food was gone Sarah and Lou were left alone with Evelyn.

"And who are you?" the question was directed at Lou.

When Lou didn't seem keen on replying Sarah spoke up.

"This is Lou, we escaped some slave traders together."

"Ah, yes. I was told that this was a possibility."

"Told by whom?" Sarah asked, confused.

"Another witch named Lily, who was told by Tanya."

"You've talked to Tanya?" Sarah exclaimed, a big smile making her face light up.

"No, not quite, I have received second-hand information as have a lot of people who have been keeping an eye and ear out in case you'd appear. Good to see you're looking pretty whole and healthy-ish."

With that Evelyn took out a small pocket mirror and handed it to Sarah:

"You know how to use this?"

Sarah nodded and eagerly accepted the mirror, chanting the words and sweeping her hand across the glass. To her delight the spell worked without any complications. The big smile on her face dimmed as someone else's face appeared in the mirror:

"You're not Tanya." The face in the mirror did look familiar but she couldn't place it.

"No, I am Luka. And you're Seraphina. When my cousin is finished in the bathroom, we'll come for you, I have your location."

"You're… Tanya's cousin?"

"Yes," he turned his face away from the mirror, as if he was listening for something, then he turned back. "We'll be with you in a moment."

Sarah was left staring at her own reflection, which looked rather dirty and wide-eyed. She sighed and handed back the mirror to Evelyn with a word of thanks. Then there was a sound like "pop" and Tanya and Luka were there. Sarah squealed and ran into her mentor's arms.

Happy reunions

They were still in Aki's house. The sun had set, and Tanya and Luka were talking with Evelyn and the other adults about something. Sera wasn't all that interested in what they were saying and was leaning against Tanya's shoulder, feeling drowsy and wanting to go home. She squinted around the room and noticed Aki sleeping against Madame Kimiko, but Lou was missing. That made Sera wake up a bit more and eventually get to her feet. Mumbling something about the bathroom she left the grownups to their conversation and went to look for her friend.

It didn't take long to find her; she was sitting in a pantry with Mr Wilkins curled up beside her. Her face was buried in her knees and Sera could hear choked sobbing.

"Lou?"

The sobbing stopped, but Lou didn't look up, instead she said with a muffled voice, "What?"

Sera sat down next to her and contemplated putting an arm around her shoulders, but instead asked: "What's wrong?"

Lou was quiet, and eventually Sera started to fidget, wondering what she should do when Lou spoke up, "I'm happy for you, you're going home with your mum." Lou lifted her head slightly, so her eyes peeked up above her kneecaps.

Sera fidgeted more, it felt weird to call Tanya her mum, but she knew that there was more Lou wanted to say.

"Okay, but why are you crying?"

There was silence a bit longer until Lou responded in a whisper which Sera had to lean in to hear.

"What's going to happen to me?"

Sera blinked.

"Well, you're coming with us of course."

Lou's head snapped up, staring at her with a surprised and almost suspicious look. The tear streaks on her face made something twist inside Sera.

"What do you mean of course?"

"Well, I mean… If you don't want to that's fine, but I don't want to just leave you…" just the thought made Sera feel slightly nauseous.

"Of course I want to come with you! But I know it's not that simple. I mean, has your mum even agreed to it?"

"Ah!" She knew there was something she'd forgotten. "Well, let's go ask her now."

With that she grabbed Lou's hand and pulled her to her feet, then they walked, Lou protesting all the while, to where the others were. Mr Wilkins followed, looking rather amused for some reason. The adults looked up as they approached. Sera was determined that Lou would be coming with them, but she still felt nervous as she stood before her mentor. Tanya looked at her curiously. Sera swallowed.

"Um… Lou's coming with us, right?"

"Is she?" Tanya's face was blank. Sera was frustrated.

"Yes! If it wasn't for her, I wouldn't have made it these last few days. Thanks to her presence I felt braver than I am. And I'm not leaving without her."

Tanya looked at her and then turned her gaze to Lou who was staring at the floor. Slowly Tanya crouched down in front of Lou:

"How do you feel about this?"

Lou shrugged, stepping closer to Sera and took hold of her arm with both hands. Tanya still managed to have eye contact with her:

"What about your parents?"

"Don't have any," Lou mumbled quietly.

Tanya sighed and stood up.

"Right."

Sera stared anxiously at her mentor as she and Luka thanked everyone in the room for their help and hospitality. Then Tanya grabbed Sera and Lou's shoulders and Luka took hold of her elbow. Before they were swept away Sera waved at Mr Wilkins who blinked at them from Evelyn's lap.

Epilogue

Tanya had said goodbye to Luka and promised to keep in touch before taking Sera and Lou home. They had taken a few days to recover from their adventures as well as getting Lou somewhat settled in. Tanya was lucky enough to have a small room for guests in her house which went to Lou, which meant the first order of business was to get the girl some clothes. That first night Tanya had found Lou in Sera's bed.

Tanya had honestly been very hesitant about taking Lou in permanently. But it hadn't taken long for her to realise that Sera and Lou had become very close in a short time, and it seemed cruel to separate them. She had got in contact with the matron of the sanctuary that Sera had been at who had offered to help her out with getting some paperwork drawn up. As a magic user she could be accused of all sorts of stuff if she didn't have papers to prove that Lou, a non-magical child, was hers.

The fact that Lou didn't exist in any systems made it simultaneously harder and easier to get the paperwork ready. Tanya decided not to question the matron's methods of getting said paperwork.

Four days after coming home they had sat down and talked about their respective adventures. It was Sera who came up with the idea that they should go around to the people who had helped her and thank them for said help. Tanya thought that was a good idea, especially considering she had promised a few of them to visit when Sera was found.

Armed with thank-you gifts they had started at Ethel's. David had just happened to be there when they arrived, and they had been invited in for tea and biscuits as David and Ethel were eager to learn what had happened after Sera had disappeared. Sera told them about her adventure and offered Ethel the small pot of flowers and box of chocolate as thanks. They had ended the visit shortly after that with Tanya offering Ethel some advice about her pains.

After that they had gone to Chloe and Leo's who looked relieved to see them, though mostly Sera, and again Sera explained what had happened after she had been transported away from them. They in turn explained what had happened after Sera, and Tanya, had gone. Apparently, their neighbour Reginald had been arrested and all his magic hunting equipment had been confiscated before he had been released back home. Their parents and several other neighbours refused to associate with him now. It was nice to hear. Sera then handed them the bottle of soda and bag of assorted sweets as a thank- you and they had insisted on sharing it with Sera and Lou as they got to know each other, with Tanya being left having to make small talk with their parents. That visit had ended with Sera becoming pen pals with Chloe and Leo and Tanya had, somehow without asking, gained a lot of parenting advice.

They had gone to the Jones' the next day and managed to intrude on a party for Mrs Jones' birthday. Everyone from that neighbourhood was there, including Flo and Aderyn. The three of them had been warmly welcomed and told to join in the festivities. Thus, the thank-you gift, flowers and chocolate again, had also become a birthday gift. Flo had appeared out of nowhere to give all of them hugs, startling poor Lou in the process. Lou and Sera had then been dragged away by Aderyn to join the other children while Tanya had ended up amongst a circle of adults discussing books. In the end they had all had a good time with good conversation, delicious cake and nice people. Lou had even come out of her shell a little bit, contributing to the conversation the children were having. And thanks to Tanya accidentally joining a book club they would definitely return there a lot.

They had gone back to thank Evelyn, Madame Kimiko, Aki and Aki's mother, Sakiko, for their part as well. The ladies in question had invited them in for tea and delicious pieces of apple pie. The atmosphere had been relaxed as Mr Wilkins purred away in Lou's lap as Tanya, Madame Kimiko and Evelyn discussed magical plants. Aki pestered Sera with questions and Lou got roped into the conversation as well. Sakiko seemed content to watch them all, occasionally contributing to either conversation. They had eventually left with promises to return soon.

Seven days after they had come home Tanya had found Luka on her doorstep, spooking her quite badly as she had opened the door to get the mail and almost ran into him. She had invited him in, though she almost regretted that as she saw Lou's reaction. The girl had gripped Sera's arm tightly and hidden behind her as best she could while staring at Luka with wide, terrified eyes. Sera had looked at Lou and then given Luka a suspicious glare. Luka in turn had looked startled, looking at the girls like he was afraid they'd bite him. Tanya had eventually broken up the standoff by grabbing Luka and leading him into another room. There they had had a short conversation, reassuring each other they were all right, before Luka left again.

Tanya had sat the girls down and gently probed Lou for information. She eventually pieced together that no, Lou had no idea who Luka was. She was just generally afraid of men. That revelation combined with the nightmares Lou had every night as well as a few odd, concerning habits of hers made Tanya determined to get some therapy for the girl. She clearly had a troubled past to work through.

Nine days after their homecoming Tanya had decided it was time to get back into routine and herded the girls into the classroom, where she had prepared a spot for Lou beforehand. She didn't really know what to teach Lou other than reading, writing and counting. So, she decided to take it as it came with the hopes that she'd come up with something new after Lou had learned the basics. Lou herself seemed excited to learn and Sera seemed more eager than usual to learn new stuff with Lou's company. Lou also didn't seem very bothered about everything magical around, which was both unexpected and a big relief.

A few days after that Tanya left the girls in the hands of a trusted neighbour and headed over to Luka's to deal with the locket once and for all. Unfortunately, it was harder to destroy than they first thought as it contained a lot of old magic and fought back. Luka eventually just put it away in a magic-proof safe in his father's old office and locked the office door for good measure.

Tanya was surprised and a bit annoyed to receive a letter from Luka via Francis shortly after that. In retaliation she answered the letter by calling him through the mirror. This started a weird communication war between them where Francis became a frequent guest, much to the girls' delight who fawned over the bird which said bird didn't seem to mind at all.

Somehow, by getting close to his familiar the girls became less wary of Luka and even came to talk to him through the mirror. This eventually led to Luka coming for a proper visit, and they visited him in turn.

They would get to the point where Luka came over regularly and helped with the girls' education. Luka's home would become a place for quality family time where the television became a big hit. The girls would call Tanya mum and Luka uncle.

There were, of course, a lot of challenges ahead for all of them before they got there. But they were all determined to overcome whatever got thrown at them.

Printed in the USA
CPSIA information can be obtained
at www.ICGtesting.com
CBHW022008190824
13414CB00027B/178